Also by Stephen King

STEPHEN KING

RITA HAYWORTH AND SHAWSHANK REDEMPTION

SCRIBNER

New York London Toronto Sydney New Delhi

Scribner

An Imprint of Simon & Schuster, Inc.

1230 Avenue of the Americas

New York, NY 10020

First Scribner trade paperback edition September 2020

For information about special discounts for bulk purchases, please contact Simon &
Schuster Special Sales at 1-866-506-1949 or business@simonandschuster.com.

The Simon & Schuster Speakers Bureau can bring authors to your live event.
For more information or to book an event, contact the Simon & Schuster Speakers Bureau
at 1-866-248-3049 or visit our website at www.simonspeakers.com.

Manufactured in the United States of America

9   10   8

ISBN 978-1-9821-5575-9

ISBN 978-1-9821-6327-3 (ebook)

For Russ and Florence Dorr

RITA HAYWORTH AND SHAWSHANK REDEMPTION

There's a guy like me in every state and federal prison in America, I guess—I'm the guy who can get it for you. Tailor-made cigarettes, a bag of reefer if you're partial to that, a bottle of brandy to celebrate your son or daughter's high school graduation, or almost anything else . . . within reason, that is. It wasn't always that way.

I came to Shawshank when I was just twenty, and I am one of the few people in our happy little family willing to own up to what they did. I committed murder. I put a large insurance policy on my wife, who was three years older than I was, and then I fixed the brakes of the Chevrolet coupe her father had given us as a wedding present. It worked out exactly as I had planned, except I hadn't planned on her stopping to pick up the neighbor woman and the neighbor woman's infant son on their way down Castle Hill and into town. The brakes let go and the car crashed through the bushes at the edge of the town common, gathering speed. Bystanders said it must have been doing fifty or better when it hit the base of the Civil War statue and burst into flames.

I also hadn't planned on getting caught, but caught I was. I got a season's pass into this place. Maine has no death-penalty, but the District Attorney saw to it that I was tried for all three deaths and given three life sentences, to run one after the other. That fixed up any chance of parole I might have for a long, long time. The judge called what I had done "a hideous, heinous crime," and it was, but it is also in the past now. You can look it up in the yellowing files of the Castle Rock *Call,* where the big headlines announcing my conviction look sort of funny and antique next to the news of Hitler and Mussolini and FDR's alphabet soup agencies.

Have I rehabilitated myself, you ask? I don't even know what that word means, at least as far as prisons and corrections go. I think it's a politician's word. It may have some other meaning, and it may be that I will have a chance to find out, but that is the future . . . something cons teach themselves not to think about. I was young, good-looking, and from the poor side of town. I knocked up a pretty, sulky, headstrong girl who lived in one of the fine old houses on Carbine Street. Her father was agreeable to the marriage if I would take a job in the optical company he owned and "work my way up." I found out that what he really had in mind was keeping me in his house and under his thumb, like a disagreeable pet that has not quite been housebroken and which may bite. Enough hate eventually piled up to cause me to do what I did. Given a second chance I would not do it again, but I'm not sure that means I am rehabilitated.

Anyway, it's not me I want to tell you about; I want to tell you about a guy named Andy Dufresne. But before I can tell you about Andy, I have to explain a few other things about myself. It won't take long.

As I said, I've been the guy who can get it for you here at Shawshank for damn near forty years. And that doesn't just mean contraband items like extra cigarettes or booze, although those items always top the list. But I've gotten thousands of other items for men doing time here, some of them perfectly legal yet hard to come by in a place where you've supposedly been brought to be punished. There was one fellow who was in for raping a little girl and exposing himself to dozens of others; I got him three pieces of pink Vermont marble and he did three lovely sculptures out of them—a baby, a boy of about twelve, and a bearded young man. He called them *The Three Ages of Jesus,* and those pieces of sculpture are now in the parlor of a man who used to be governor of this state.

Or here's a name you may remember if you grew up north of Massachusetts—Robert Alan Cote. In 1951 he tried to rob the First Mercantile Bank of Mechanic Falls, and the holdup turned into a bloodbath—six dead in the end, two of them members of the gang, three of them hostages, one of them a young state cop who put his head up at the wrong time and got a bullet in the eye. Cote had a penny collection. Naturally they weren't going to let him have it in here, but with a little help from his mother and a middleman who used to drive a laundry truck, I was able to get it for him. I told him, Bobby, you must be crazy, wanting to have a coin collection in a stone hotel full of thieves. He looked at me and smiled and said, I know where to keep them. They'll be safe enough. Don't you worry. And he was right. Bobby Cote died of a brain tumor in 1967, but that coin collection has never turned up.

I've gotten men chocolates on Valentine's Day; I got three of those green milkshakes they serve at McDonald's around St. Paddy's Day for a crazy Irishman named O'Malley; I even arranged for a midnight showing of *Deep Throat* and *The Devil in Miss Jones* for a party of twenty men who had pooled their resources to rent the films . . . although I ended up doing a week in solitary for that little escapade. It's the risk you run when you're the guy who can get it.

I've gotten reference books and fuck-books, joke novelties like handbuzzers and itching powder, and on more than one occasion I've seen that a long-timer has gotten a pair of panties from his wife or his girlfriend . . . and I guess you'll know what guys in here do with such items during the long nights when time draws out like a blade. I don't get all those things gratis, and for some items the price comes high. But I don't do it *just* for the money; what good is money to me? I'm never going to own a Cadillac car or fly off to Jamaica for two weeks in February. I do it for the same reason that a good butcher will only sell you fresh meat: I got a reputation and I want to keep it. The only two things I refuse to handle are guns and heavy drugs. I won't help anyone kill himself or anyone else. I have enough killing on my mind to last me a lifetime.

Yeah, I'm a regular Neiman-Marcus. And so when Andy Dufresne came to me in 1949 and asked if I could smuggle Rita Hayworth into the prison for him, I said it would be no problem at all. And it wasn't.

When Andy came to Shawshank in 1948, he was thirty years old. He was a short, neat little man with sandy hair and small, clever hands. He wore gold-rimmed spectacles. His finger-nails were always clipped, and they were always clean. That's a funny thing to remember about a man, I suppose, but it seems to sum Andy up for me. He always looked as if he should have been wearing a tie. On the outside he had been a vice-president in the trust department of a large Portland bank. Good work for a man as young as he was especially when you consider how conservative most banks are . . . and you have to multiply that conservatism by ten when you get up into New England, where folks don't like to trust a man with their money unless he's bald, limping, and constantly plucking at his pants to get his truss around straight. Andy was in for murdering his wife and her lover.

As I believe I have said, everyone in prison is an innocent man. Oh, they read that scripture the way those holy rollers on TV read the Book of Revelation. They were the victims of judges with hearts of stone and balls to match, or incompetent lawyers, or police frame-ups, or bad luck. They read the scrip-ture, but you can see a different scripture in their faces. Most cons are a low sort, no good to themselves or anyone else, and their worst luck was that their mothers carried them to term.

In all my years at Shawshank, there have been less than ten

men whom I believed when they told me they were innocent. Andy Dufresne was one of them, although I only became convinced of his innocence over a period of years. If I had been on that jury that heard his case in Portland Superior Court over six stormy weeks in 1947–48, I would have voted to convict, too.

It was one hell of a case, all right; one of those juicy ones with all the right elements. There was a beautiful girl with society connections (dead), a local sports figure (also dead), and a prominent young businessman in the dock. There was this, plus all the scandal the newspapers could hint at. The prosecution had an open-and-shut case. The trial only lasted as long as it did because the DA was planning to run for the U.S. House of Representatives and he wanted John Q. Public to get a good long look at his phiz. It was a crackerjack legal circus, with spectators getting in line at four in the morning, despite the subzero temperatures, to assure themselves of a seat.

The facts of the prosecution's case that Andy never contested were these: that he had a wife, Linda Collins Dufresne; that in June of 1947 she had expressed an interest in learning the game of golf at the Falmouth Hills Country Club; that she did indeed take lessons for four months; that her instructor was the Falmouth Hills golf pro, Glenn Quentin; that in late August of 1947 Andy learned that Quentin and his wife had become lovers; that Andy and Linda Dufresne argued bitterly on the afternoon of September 10th, 1947; that the subject of their argument was her infidelity.

He testified that Linda professed to be glad he knew; the sneaking around, she said, was distressing. She told Andy that she planned to obtain a Reno divorce. Andy told her he would see her in hell before he would see her in Reno. She went off to spend the night with Quentin in Quentin's rented bungalow not far from the golf course. The next morning his cleaning woman found both of them dead in bed. Each had been shot four times.

It was that last fact that militated more against Andy than any of the others. The DA with the political aspirations made a great deal of it in his opening statement and his closing summation. Andrew Dufresne, he said, was not a wronged husband seeking a hot-blooded revenge against his cheating wife; that, the DA said, could be understood, if not condoned. But this revenge had been of a much colder type. Consider! the DA thundered at the jury. Four and four! Not six shots, but eight! *He had fired the gun empty . . . and then stopped to reload so he could shoot each of them again!* FOUR FOR HIM AND FOUR FOR HER, the Portland *Sun* blared. The Boston *Register* dubbed him The Even-Steven Killer.

A clerk from the Wise Pawnshop in Lewiston testified that he had sold a six-shot .38 Police Special to Andrew Dufresne just two days before the double murder. A bartender from the country club bar testified that Andy had come in around seven o'clock on the evening of September 10th, had tossed off three straight whiskeys in a twenty-minute period—when he got up from the bar-stool he told the bartender that he was going up to Glenn Quentin's house and he, the bartender, could "read about the rest of it in the papers." Another clerk, this one from the Handy-Pik store a mile or so from Quentin's house, told the court that Dufresne had come in around quarter to nine on that same night. He purchased cigarettes, three quarts of beer, and some dishtowels. The county medical examiner testified that Quentin and the Dufresne woman had been killed between 11:00 p.m. and 2:00 a.m. on the night of September 10th–11th. The detective from the Attorney General's office who had been in charge of the case testified that there was a turnout less than seventy yards from the bungalow, and that on the afternoon of September 11th, three pieces of evidence had been removed from that turnout: first item, two empty quart bottles of Narragansett Beer (with the defendant's fingerprints on them); second item, twelve cigarette ends (all Kools, the defendant's brand); third item, a plaster moulage of a set of tire tracks (exactly matching the tread-and-wear pattern of the tires on the defendant's 1947 Plymouth).

In the living room of Quentin's bungalow, four dishtowels had been found lying on the sofa. There were bullet-holes through them and powder-burns on them. The detective theorized (over the agonized objections of Andy's lawyer) that the murderer had wrapped the towels around the muzzle of the murder-weapon to muffle the sound of the gunshots.

Andy Dufresne took the stand in his own defense and told his story calmly, coolly, and dispassionately. He said he had begun to hear distressing rumors about his wife and Glenn Quentin as early as the last week in July. In late August he had become distressed enough to investigate a bit. On an evening when Linda was supposed to have gone shopping in Portland after her golf lesson, Andy had followed her and Quentin to Quentin's one-story rented house (inevitably dubbed "the love-nest" by the papers). He had parked in the turnout until Quentin drove her back to the country club where her car was parked, about three hours later.

"Do you mean to tell this court that you followed your wife in your brand-new Plymouth sedan?" the DA asked him on cross-examination.

"I swapped cars for the evening with a friend," Andy said, and this cool admission of how well-planned his investigation had been did him no good at all in the eyes of the jury.

After returning the friend's car and picking up his own, he had gone home. Linda had been in bed, reading a book. He asked her how her trip to Portland had been. She replied that it had been fun, but she hadn't seen anything she liked well enough to buy. "That's when I knew for sure," Andy told the breathless spectators. He spoke in the same calm, remote voice in which he delivered almost all of his testimony.

"What was your frame of mind in the seventeen days between then and the night your wife was murdered?" Andy's lawyer asked him.

"I was in great distress," Andy said calmly, coldly. Like a man reciting a shopping list he said that he had considered suicide, and had even gone so far as to purchase a gun in Lewiston on September 8th.

His lawyer then invited him to tell the jury what had happened after his wife left to meet Glenn Quentin on the night of the murders. Andy told them . . . and the impression he made was the worst possible.

I knew him for close to thirty years, and I can tell you he was the most self-possessed man I've ever known. What was right with him he'd only give you a little at a time. What was wrong with him he kept bottled up inside. If he ever had a dark night of the soul, as some writer or other has called it, you would never know. He was the type of man who, if he had decided to commit suicide, would do it without leaving a note but not until his affairs had been put neatly in order. If he had cried on the witness stand, or if his voice had thickened and grown hesitant, even if he had started yelling at that Washington-bound District Attorney, I don't believe he would have gotten the life sentence he wound up with. Even if he had've, he would have been out on parole by 1954. But he told his story like a recording machine, seeming to say to the jury: This is it. Take it or leave it. They left it.

He said he was drunk that night, that he'd been more or less drunk since August 24th, and that he was a man who didn't handle his liquor very well. Of course that by itself would have been hard for any jury to swallow. They just couldn't see this coldly self-possessed young man in the neat double-breasted three-piece woollen suit ever getting falling-down drunk over his wife's sleazy little affair with some small-town golf pro. I believed it because I had a chance to watch Andy that those six men and six women didn't have.

Andy Dufresne took just four drinks a year all the time I knew him. He would meet me in the exercise yard every year about a week before his birthday and then again about two weeks before Christmas. On each occasion he would arrange for a bottle of Jack Daniel's. He bought it the way most cons arrange to buy their stuff—the slave's wages they pay in here, plus a little of his own. Up until 1965 what you got for your time was a dime an hour. In '65 they raised it all the way up to a quarter. My commission on liquor was and is ten per cent, and when you add on that surcharge to the price of a fine sippin whiskey like the Black Jack, you get an idea of how many hours of Andy Dufresne's sweat in the prison laundry was going to buy his four drinks a year.

On the morning of his birthday, September 20th, he would have himself a big knock, and then he'd have another that night after lights-out. The following day he'd give the rest of the bottle back to me, and I would share it around. As for the other bottle, he dealt himself one drink Christmas night and another on New Year's Eve. Then that bottle would also come to me with instructions to pass it on. Four drinks a year—and that is the behavior of a man who has been bitten hard by the bottle. Hard enough to draw blood.

He told the jury that on the night of the tenth he had been so drunk he could only remember what had happened in little isolated snatches. He had gotten drunk that afternoon—"I took on a double helping of Dutch courage" is how he put it—before taking on Linda.

After she left to meet Quentin, he remembered deciding to confront them. On the way to Quentin's bungalow, he swung into the country club for a couple of quick ones. He could not, he said, remember telling the bartender he could "read about the rest of it in the papers," or saying anything to him at all. He remembered buying beer in the Handy-Pik, but not the dishtowels. "Why would I want dishtowels?" he asked, and one of the papers reported that three of the lady jurors shuddered.

Later, much later, he speculated to me about the clerk who had testified on the subject of those dishtowels, and I think it's worth jotting down what he said. "Suppose that, during their canvass for witnesses," Andy said one day in the exercise yard, "they stumble on this fellow who sold me the beer that night. By then three days have gone by. The facts of the case have been broadsided in all the papers. Maybe they ganged up on the guy, five or six cops, plus the dick from the Attorney General's office, plus the DA's assistant. Memory is a pretty subjective thing, Red. They could have started out with 'Isn't it possible that he purchased four or five dishtowels?' and worked their way up from there. If enough people *want* you to remember something, that can be a pretty powerful persuader."

I agreed that it could.

"But there's one even more powerful," Andy went on in that musing way of his. "I think it's at least possible that he convinced himself. It was the limelight. Reporters asking him questions, his picture in the papers . . . all topped, of course, by his star turn in court. I'm not saying that he deliberately falsified his story, or perjured himself. I think it's possible that he could have passed a lie detector test with flying colors, or sworn on his mother's sacred name that I bought those dishtowels. But still . . . memory is such a *goddam* subjective thing.

"I know this much: even though my own lawyer thought I had to be lying about half my story, he never bought that business about the dishtowels. It's crazy on the face of it. I was pig-drunk, too drunk to have been thinking about muffling the gunshots. If I'd done it, I just would have let them rip."

He went up to the turnout and parked there. He drank beer and smoked cigarettes. He watched the lights downstairs in Quentin's place go out. He watched a single light go on upstairs . . . and fifteen minutes later he watched that one go out. He said he could guess the rest.

"Mr. Dufresne, did you then go up to Glenn Quentin's house and kill the two of them?" his lawyer thundered.

"No, I did not," Andy answered. By midnight, he said, he was sobering up. He was also feeling the first signs of a bad hangover. He decided to go home and sleep it off and think about the whole thing in a more adult fashion the next day. "At that time, as I drove home, I was beginning to think that the wisest course would be to simply let her go to Reno and get her divorce."

"Thank you, Mr. Dufresne."

The DA popped up.

"You divorced her in the quickest way you could think of, didn't you? You divorced her with a .38 revolver wrapped in dishtowels, didn't you?"

"No, sir, I did not," Andy said calmly.

"And then you shot her lover."

"No, sir."

"You mean you shot Quentin first?"

"I mean I didn't shoot either one of them. I drank two quarts of beer and smoked however many cigarettes the police found at the turnout. Then I drove home and went to bed."

"You told the jury that between August twenty-fourth and September tenth you were feeling suicidal."

"Yes, sir."

"Suicidal enough to buy a revolver."

"Yes."

"Would it bother you overmuch, Mr. Dufresne, if I told you that you do not seem to me to be the suicidal type?"

"No," Andy said, "but you don't impress me as being terribly sensitive, and I doubt very much that, if I *were* feeling suicidal, I would take my problem to you."

There was a slight tense titter in the courtroom at this, but it won him no points with the jury.

"Did you take your thirty-eight with you on the night of September tenth?"

"No; as I've already testified—"

"Oh, yes!" The DA smiled sarcastically. "You threw it into the river, didn't you? The Royal River. On the afternoon of September ninth."

11

"Yes, sir."

"One day before the murders."

"Yes, sir."

"That's convenient, isn't it?"

"It's neither convenient nor inconvenient. Only the truth."

"I believe you heard Lieutenant Mincher's testimony?" Mincher had been in charge of the party which had dragged the stretch of the Royal near Pond Road Bridge, from which Andy had testified he had thrown the gun. The police had not found it.

"Yes, sir. You know I heard it."

"Then you heard him tell the court that they found no gun, although they dragged for three days. That was rather convenient, too, wasn't it?"

"Convenience aside, it's a fact that they didn't find the gun," Andy responded calmly. "But I should like to point out to both you and the jury that the Pond Road Bridge is very close to where the Royal River empties into the Bay of Yarmouth. The current is strong. The gun may have been carried out into the bay itself."

"And so no comparison can be made between the riflings on the bullets taken from the bloodstained corpses of your wife and Mr. Glenn Quentin and the riflings on the barrel of your gun. That's correct, isn't it, Mr. Dufresne?"

"Yes."

"That's also rather convenient, isn't it?"

At that, according to the papers, Andy displayed one of the few slight emotional reactions he allowed himself during the entire six-week period of the trial. A slight, bitter smile crossed his face.

"Since I am innocent of this crime, sir, and since I am telling the truth about throwing my gun into the river the day before the crime took place, then it seems to me decidedly inconvenient that the gun was never found."

The DA hammered at him for two days. He re-read the

Handy-Pik clerk's testimony about the dishtowels to Andy. Andy repeated that he could not recall buying them, but admitted that he also couldn't remember *not* buying them.

Was it true that Andy and Linda Dufresne had taken out a joint insurance policy in early 1947? Yes, that was true. And if acquitted, wasn't it true that Andy stood to gain fifty thousand dollars in benefits? True. And wasn't it true that he had gone up to Glenn Quentin's house with murder in his heart, and wasn't it *also* true that he had indeed committed murder twice over? No, it was not true. Then what did he think had happened, since there had been no signs of robbery?

"I have no way of knowing that, sir," Andy said quietly.

The case went to the jury at 1:00 p.m. on a snowy Wednesday afternoon. The twelve jurymen and -women came back in at 3:30. The bailiff said they would have been back earlier, but they had held off in order to enjoy a nice chicken dinner from Bentley's Restaurant at the county's expense. They found him guilty, and brother, if Maine had the death-penalty, he would have done the airdance before that spring's crocuses poked their heads out of the snow.

The DA had asked him what he thought had happened, and Andy slipped the question—but he did have an idea, and I got it out of him late one evening in 1955. It had taken those seven years for us to progress from nodding acquaintances to fairly close friends—but I never felt really close to Andy until 1960 or so, and I believe I was the only one who ever did get really close to him. Both being long-timers, we were in the same cellblock from beginning to end, although I was halfway down the corridor from him.

"What do I think?" He laughed—but there was no humor in the sound. "I think there was a lot of bad luck floating around that night. More than could ever get together in the same short span of time again. I think it must have been some stranger, just passing through. Maybe someone who had a flat tire on that road after I went home. Maybe a burglar. Maybe a psychopath. He killed them, that's all. And I'm here."

As simple as that. And he was condemned to spend the rest of his life in Shawshank—or the part of it that mattered. Five years later he began to have parole hearings, and he was turned down just as regular as clockwork in spite of being a model prisoner. Getting a pass out of Shawshank when you've got *murder* stamped on your admittance-slip is slow work, as slow as a river eroding a rock. Seven men sit on the board, two more than at most state prisons, and every one of those seven has an ass as hard as the water drawn up from a mineral-spring well. You can't buy those guys, you can't sweet-talk them, you can't cry for them. As far as the board in here is concerned, money don't talk, and *nobody* walks. There were other reasons in Andy's case as well . . . but that belongs a little further along in my story.

There was a trusty, name of Kendricks, who was into me for some pretty heavy money back in the fifties, and it was four years before he got it all paid off. Most of the interest he paid me was information—in my line of work, you're dead if you can't find ways of keeping your ear to the ground. This Kendricks, for instance, had access to records I was never going to see running a stamper down in the goddam plate-shop.

Kendricks told me that the parole board vote was 7-0 against Andy Dufresne through 1957, 6-1 in '58; 7-0 again in '59, and 5-2 in '60. After that I don't know, but I do know that sixteen years later he was still in Cell 14 of Cellblock 5. By then, 1975, he was fifty-seven. They probably would have gotten big-hearted and let him out around 1983. They give you life, and that's what they take—all of it that counts, any-way. Maybe they set you loose someday, but . . . well, listen: I knew this guy, Sherwood Bolton, his name was, and he had this pigeon in his cell. From 1945 until 1953, when they let him out, he had that pigeon. He wasn't any Birdman of Alca-traz; he just had this pigeon. Jake, he called him. He set Jake free a day before he, Sherwood, that is, was to walk, and Jake flew away just as pretty as you could want. But about a week after Sherwood Bolton left our happy little family, a friend of mine called me over to the west corner of the exercise yard, where Sherwood used to hang out. A bird was lying there like a very small pile of dirty bedlinen. It looked starved. My friend said: "Isn't that Jake, Red?" It was. That pigeon was just as dead as a turd.

I remember the first time Andy Dufresne got in touch with me for something; I remember like it was yesterday. That wasn't the time he wanted Rita Hayworth, though. That came later. In the summer of 1948 he came around for something else.

Most of my deals are done right there in the exercise yard, and that's where this one went down. Our yard is big, much bigger than most. It's a perfect square, ninety yards on a side. The north side is the outer wall, with a guard-tower at either end. The guards up there are armed with binoculars and riot guns. The main gate is in that north side. The truck loading-bays are on the south side of the yard. There are five of them. Shawshank is a busy place during the work-week—deliveries in, deliveries out. We have the license-plate factory, and a big industrial laundry that does all the prison wetwash, plus that of Kittery Receiving Hospital and the Eliot Nursing Home. There's also a big automotive garage where mechanic inmates fix prison, state, and municipal vehicles—not to mention the private cars of the screws, the administration offices . . . and, on more than one occasion, those of the parole board.

The east side is a thick stone wall full of tiny slit windows. Cellblock 5 is on the other side of that wall. The west side is Administration and the infirmary. Shawshank has never been as overcrowded as most prisons, and back in '48 it was only filled to something like two-thirds capacity, but at any given time there might be eighty to a hundred and twenty cons on the yard—playing toss with a football or baseball, shooting craps, jawing at each other, making deals. On Sunday the place was even more crowded; on Sunday the place would have looked like a country holiday . . . if there had been any women.

It was on a Sunday that Andy first came to me. I had just finished talking to Elmore Armitage, a fellow who often came in handy to me, about a radio when Andy walked up. I knew who he was, of course; he had a reputation for being a snob and a cold fish. People were saying he was marked for trouble already. One of the people saying so was Bogs Diamond, a bad man to have on your case. Andy had no cellmate, and I'd heard that was just the way he wanted it, although people were already saying he thought his shit smelled sweeter than the ordinary. But I don't have to listen to rumors about a man when I can judge him for myself.

"Hello," he said. "I'm Andy Dufresne." He offered his hand and I shook it. He wasn't a man to waste time being social; he got right to the point. "I understand that you're a man who knows how to get things."

I agreed that I was able to locate certain items from time to time.

"How do you do that?" Andy asked.

"Sometimes," I said, "things just seem to come into my hand. I can't explain it. Unless it's because I'm Irish."

He smiled a little at that. "I wonder if you could get me a rock-hammer."

"What would that be, and why would you want it?"

Andy looked surprised. "Do you make motivations a part of your business?" With words like those I could understand how he had gotten a reputation for being the snobby sort, the kind of guy who likes to put on airs—but I sensed a tiny thread of humor in his question.

"I'll tell you," I said. "If you wanted a toothbrush, I wouldn't ask questions. I'd just quote you a price. Because a toothbrush, you see, is a non-lethal sort of an object."

"You have strong feelings about lethal objects?"

"I do."

An old friction-taped baseball flew toward us and he turned, cat-quick, and picked it out of the air. It was a move Frank Malzone would have been proud of. Andy flicked the ball back to where it had come from—just a quick and easy-looking flick of the wrist, but that throw had some mustard on it, just the same. I could see a lot of people were watching us with one eye as they went about their business. Probably the guards in the tower were watching, too. I won't gild the lily; there are cons that swing weight in any prison, maybe four or five in a small one, maybe two or three dozen in a big one. At Shawshank I was one of those with some weight, and what I thought of Andy Dufresne would have a lot to do with how his time went. He probably knew it, too, but he wasn't kowtowing or sucking up to me, and I respected him for that.

"Fair enough. I'll tell you what it is and why I want it. A rock-hammer looks like a miniature pickaxe—about so long." He held his hands about a foot apart, and that was when I first noticed how neatly kept his nails were. "It's got a small sharp pick on one end and a flat, blunt hammerhead on the other. I want it because I like rocks."

"Rocks," I said.

"Squat down here a minute," he said.

I humored him. We hunkered down on our haunches like Indians.

Andy took a handful of exercise yard dirt and began to sift it between his neat hands, so it emerged in a fine cloud. Small pebbles were left over, one or two sparkly, the rest dull and plain. One of the dull ones was quartz, but it was only dull until you'd rubbed it clean. Then it had a nice milky glow. Andy did the cleaning and then tossed it to me. I caught it and named it.

"Quartz, sure," he said. "And look. Mica. Shale. Silted granite. Here's a piece of graded limestone, from when they cut this place out of the side of the hill." He tossed them away and dusted his hands. "I'm a rockhound. At least. . . I *was* a rockhound. In my old life. I'd like to be one again, on a limited scale."

"Sunday expeditions in the exercise yard?" I asked, standing up. It was a silly idea, and yet . . . seeing that little piece of quartz had given my heart a funny tweak. I don't know exactly why; just an association with the outside world, I suppose. You didn't think of such things in terms of the yard. Quartz was something you picked out of a small, quick-running stream.

"Better to have Sunday expeditions here than no Sunday expeditions at all," he said.

"You could plant an item like that rock-hammer in somebody's skull," I remarked.

"I have no enemies here," he said quietly.

"No?" I smiled. "Wait awhile."

"If there's trouble, I can handle it without using a rock-hammer."

"Maybe you want to try an escape? Going under the wall? Because if you do—"

He laughed politely. When I saw the rock-hammer three weeks later, I understood why.

"You know," I said, "if anyone sees you with it, they'll take it away. If they saw you with a spoon, they'd take it away. What are you going to do, just sit down here in the yard and start bangin away?"

"Oh, I believe I can do a lot better than that."

I nodded. That part of it really wasn't my business, anyway. A man engages my services to get him something. Whether he can keep it or not after I get it is his business.

"How much would an item like that go for?" I asked. I was beginning to enjoy his quiet, low-key style. When you've spent ten years in stir, as I had then, you can get awfully tired of the bellowers and the braggarts and the loud-mouths. Yes, I think it would be fair to say I liked Andy from the first.

"Eight dollars in any rock-and-gem shop," he said, "but I

realize that in a business like yours you work on a cost-plus basis—"

"Cost plus ten per cent is my going rate, but I have to go up some on a dangerous item. For something like the gadget you're talking about, it takes a little more goose-grease to get the wheels turning. Let's say ten dollars."

"Ten it is."

I looked at him, smiling a little. "Have you *got* ten dollars?"

"I do," he said quietly.

A long time after, I discovered that he had better than five hundred. He had brought it in with him. When they check you in at this hotel, one of the bellhops is obliged to bend you over and take a look up your works—but there are a lot of works, and, not to put too fine a point on it, a man who is really determined can get a fairly large item quite a ways up them—far enough to be out of sight, unless the bellhop you happen to draw is in the mood to pull on a rubber glove and go prospecting.

"That's fine," I said. "You ought to know what I expect if you get caught with what I get you."

"I suppose I should," he said, and I could tell by the slight change in his gray eyes that he knew exactly what I was going to say. It was a slight lightening, a gleam of his special ironic humor.

"If you get caught, you'll say you found it. That's about the long and short of it. They'll put you in solitary for three or four weeks . . . plus, of course, you'll lose your toy and you'll get a black mark on your record. If you give them my name, you and I will never do business again. Not for so much as a pair of shoelaces or a bag of Bugler. And I'll send some fellows around to lump you up. I don't like violence, but you'll understand my position. I can't allow it to get around that I can't handle myself. That would surely finish me."

"Yes. I suppose it would. I understand, and you don't need to worry."

"I never worry," I said. "In a place like this there's no percentage in it."

He nodded and walked away. Three days later he walked up beside me in the exercise yard during the laundry's morning break. He didn't speak or even look my way, but pressed a picture of the Hon. Alexander Hamilton into my hand as neatly as a good magician does a card-trick. He was a man who adapted fast. I got him his rock-hammer. I had it in my cell for one night, and it was just as he described it. It was no tool for escape (it would have taken a man just about six hundred years to tunnel under the wall using that rock-hammer, I figured), but I still felt some misgivings. If you planted that pickaxe end in a man's head, he would surely never listen to *Fibber McGee and Molly* on the radio again. And Andy had already begun having trouble with the sisters. I hoped it wasn't them he was wanting the rock-hammer for.

In the end, I trusted my judgment. Early the next morning, twenty minutes before the wake-up horn went off, I slipped the rock-hammer and a package of Camels to Ernie, the old trusty who swept the Cellblock 5 corridors until he was let free in 1956. He slipped it into his tunic without a word, and I didn't see the rock-hammer again for nineteen years, and by then it was damned near worn away to nothing.

The following Sunday Andy walked over to me in the exercise yard again. He was nothing to look at that day, I can tell you. His lower lip was swelled up so big it looked like a summer sausage, his right eye was swollen half-shut, and there was an ugly washboard scrape across one cheek. He was having his troubles with the sisters, all right, but he never mentioned them. "Thanks for the tool," he said, and walked away.

I watched him curiously. He walked a few steps, saw something in the dirt, bent over, and picked it up. It was a small rock. Prison fatigues, except for those worn by mechanics when they're on the job, have no pockets. But there are ways to get around that. The little pebble disappeared up Andy's sleeve and didn't come down. I admired that . . . and I admired him. In spite of the problems he was having, he was going on with his life. There are thousands who don't or won't or can't, and plenty of them aren't in prison, either. And I noticed that, although his face looked as if a twister had happened to it, his hands were still neat and clean, the nails well-kept.

I didn't see much of him over the next six months; Andy spent a lot of that time in solitary.

A few words about the sisters.

In a lot of pens they are known as bull queers or jailhouse susies—just lately the term in fashion is "killer queens." But in Shawshank they were always the sisters. I don't know why, but other than the name I guess there was no difference.

It comes as no surprise to most these days that there's a lot of buggery going on inside the walls—except to some of the new fish, maybe, who have the misfortune to be young, slim, good-looking, and unwary—but homosexuality, like straight sex, comes in a hundred different shapes and forms. There are men who can't stand to be without sex of some kind and turn to another man to keep from going crazy. Usually what follows is an arrangement between two fundamentally heterosexual men, although I've sometimes wondered if they are quite as heterosexual as they thought they were going to be when they get back to their wives or their girlfriends.

There are also men who get "turned" in prison. In the current parlance they "go gay," or "come out of the closet." Mostly (but not always) they play the female, and their favors are competed for fiercely.

And then there are the sisters.

They are to prison society what the rapist is to the society outside the walls. They're usually long-timers, doing hard bullets for brutal crimes. Their prey is the young, the weak, and the inexperienced . . . or, as in the case of Andy Dufresne, the weak-looking. Their hunting grounds are the showers, the cramped, tunnel-like areaway behind the industrial washers in the laundry, sometimes the infirmary. On more than one occasion rape has occurred in the closet-sized projection booth behind the auditorium. Most often what the sisters take by force they could have had for free, if they wanted it that way; those who have been turned always seem to have "crushes" on one sister or another, like teenage girls with their Sinatras, Presleys, or Redfords. But for the sisters, the joy has always been in taking it by force . . . and I guess it always will be.

Because of his small size and fair good looks (and maybe also because of that very quality of self-possession I had admired), the sisters were after Andy from the day he walked in. If this was some kind of fairy story, I'd tell you that Andy fought the good fight until they left him alone. I wish I could say that, but I can't. Prison is no fairy-tale world.

The first time for him was in the shower less than three days after he joined our happy Shawshank family. Just a lot of slap and tickle that time, I understand. They like to size you up before they make their real move, like jackals finding out if the prey is as weak and hamstrung as it looks.

Andy punched back and bloodied the lip of a big, hulking sister named Bogs Diamond—gone these many years since to who knows where. A guard broke it up before it could go any further, but Bogs promised to get him—and Bogs did.

The second time was behind the washers in the laundry. A lot has gone on in that long, dusty, and narrow space over the years; the guards know about it and just let it be. It's dim and littered with bags of washing and bleaching compound, drums of Hexlite catalyst, as harmless as salt if your hands are dry, murderous as battery acid if they're wet. The guards don't like to go back there. There's no room to maneuver, and one of the first things they teach them when they come to work in a place like this is to never let the cons get you in a place where you can't back up.

Bogs wasn't there that day, but Henley Backus, who had been

washroom foreman down there since 1922, told me that four of his friends were. Andy held them at bay for awhile with a scoop of Hexlite, threatening to throw it in their eyes if they came any closer, but he tripped trying to back around one of the big Washex four-pockets. That was all it took. They were on him.

I guess the phrase gang-rape is one that doesn't change much from one generation to the next. That's what they did to him, those four sisters. They bent him over a gear-box and one of them held a Phillips screwdriver to his temple while they gave him the business. It rips you up some, but not bad—am I speaking from personal experience, you ask?—I only wish I weren't. You bleed for awhile. If you don't want some clown asking you if you just started your period, you wad up a bunch of toilet paper and keep it down the back of your underwear until it stops. The bleeding really is like a menstrual flow; it keeps up for two, maybe three days, a slow trickle. Then it stops. No harm done, unless they've done something even more unnatural to you. No *physical* harm done—but rape is rape, and eventually you have to look at your face in the mirror again and decide what to make of yourself.

Andy went through that alone, the way he went through everything alone in those days. He must have come to the conclusion that others before him had come to, namely, that there are only two ways to deal with the sisters: fight them and get taken, or just get taken.

He decided to fight. When Bogs and two of his buddies came after him a week or so after the laundry incident ("I heard ya got broke in," Bogs said, according to Ernie, who was around at the time), Andy slugged it out with them. He broke the nose of a fellow named Rooster MacBride, a heavy-gutted farmer who was in for beating his stepdaughter to death. Rooster died in here, I'm happy to add.

They took him, all three of them. When it was done, Rooster and the other egg—it might have been Pete Verness, but I'm not completely sure—forced Andy down to his knees. Bogs

Diamond stepped in front of him. He had a pearl-handled razor in those days with the words *Diamond Pearl* engraved on both sides of the grip. He opened it and said, "I'm gonna open my fly now, mister man, and you're going to swallow what I give you to swallow. And when you done swallowed mine, you're gonna swallow Rooster's. I guess you done broke his nose and I think he ought to have something to pay for it."

Andy said, "Anything of yours that you stick in my mouth, you're going to lose it."

Bogs looked at Andy like he was crazy, Ernie said.

"No," he told Andy, talking to him slowly, like Andy was a stupid kid. "You didn't understand what I said. You do anything like that and I'll put all eight inches of this steel into your ear. Get it?"

"I understood what you said. I don't think you understood *me.* I'm going to bite whatever you stick into my mouth. You can put that razor into my brain, I guess, but you should know that a sudden serious brain injury causes the victim to simultaneously urinate, defecate . . . and bite down."

He looked up at Bogs smiling that little smile of his, old Ernie said, as if the three of them had been discussing stocks and bonds with him instead of throwing it to him just as hard as they could. Just as if he was wearing one of his three-piece bankers' suits instead of kneeling on a dirty broom-closet floor with his pants around his ankles and blood trickling down the insides of his thighs.

"In fact," he went on, "I understand that the bite-reflex is sometimes so strong that the victim's jaws have to be pried open with a crowbar or a jackhandle."

Bogs didn't put anything in Andy's mouth that night in late February of 1948, and neither did Rooster MacBride, and so far as I know, no one else ever did, either. What the three of them did was to beat Andy within an inch of his life, and all four of them ended up doing a jolt in solitary. Andy and Rooster MacBride went by way of the infirmary.

How many times did that particular crew have at him? I don't know. I think Rooster lost his taste fairly early on—being in nose-splints for a month can do that to a fellow—and Bogs Diamond left off that summer, all at once.

That was a strange thing. Bogs was found in his cell, badly beaten, one morning in early June, when he didn't show up in the breakfast nose-count. He wouldn't say who had done it, or how they had gotten to him, but being in my business, I know that a screw can be bribed to do almost anything except get a gun for an inmate. They didn't make big salaries then, and they don't now. And in those days there was no electronic locking system, no closed-circuit TV, no master-switches which controlled whole areas of the prison. Back in 1948, each cell-block had its own turnkey. A guard could have been bribed real easy to let someone—maybe two or three someones—into the block, and, yes, even into Diamond's cell.

Of course a job like that would have cost a lot of money. Not by outside standards, no. Prison economics are on a smaller scale. When you've been in here awhile, a dollar bill in your hand looks like a twenty did outside. My guess is that, if Bogs was done, it cost someone a serious piece of change—fifteen bucks, we'll say, for the turnkey, and two or three apiece for each of the lump-up guys.

I'm not saying it was Andy Dufresne, but I do know that he brought in five hundred dollars when he came, and he was a banker in the straight world—a man who understands better than the rest of us the ways in which money can become power.

And I know this: after the beating—the three broken ribs, the hemorrhaged eye, the sprained back, and the dislocated hip—Bogs Diamond left Andy alone. In fact, after that he left everyone pretty much alone. He got to be like a high wind in the summertime, all bluster and no bite. You could say, in fact, that he turned into a "weak sister."

• • •

That was the end of Bogs Diamond, a man who might eventually have killed Andy if Andy hadn't taken steps to prevent it (if it *was* him who took the steps). But it wasn't the end of Andy's troubles with the sisters. There was a little hiatus, and then it began again, although not so hard or so often. Jackals like easy prey, and there were easier pickings around than Andy Dufresne.

He always fought them, that's what I remember. He knew, I guess, that if you let them have at you even once without fighting, it got that much easier to let them have their way without fighting next time. So Andy would turn up with bruises on his face every once in awhile, and there was the matter of the two broken fingers six or eight months after Diamond's beating. Oh yes—and sometime in late 1949, the man landed in the infirmary with a broken cheekbone that was probably the result of someone swinging a nice chunk of pipe with the business-end wrapped in flannel. He always fought back, and as a result, he did his time in solitary. But I don't think solitary was the hardship for Andy that it was for some men. He got along with himself.

The sisters was something he adjusted himself to—and then, in 1950, it stopped almost completely. That is a part of my story that I'll get to in due time.

In the fall of 1948, Andy met me one morning in the exercise yard and asked me if I could get him half a dozen rock-blankets.

"What the hell are those?" I asked.

He told me that was just what rockhounds called them; they were polishing cloths about the size of dishtowels. They were heavily padded, with a smooth side and a rough side— the smooth side like fine-grained sandpaper, the rough side almost as abrasive as industrial steel wool (Andy also kept a box of that in his cell, although he didn't get it from me—I imagine he kited it from the prison laundry).

I told him I thought we could do business on those, and I ended up getting them from the very same rock-and-gem shop where I'd arranged to get the rock-hammer. This time I charged Andy my usual ten per cent and not a penny more. I didn't see anything lethal or even dangerous in a dozen 7" x 7" squares of padded cloth. Rock-blankets, indeed.

It was about five months later that Andy asked if I could get him Rita Hayworth. That conversation took place in the auditorium, during a movie-show. Nowadays we get the movie-shows once or twice a week, but back then the shows were a monthly event. Usually the movies we got had a morally uplifting message to them, and this one, *The Lost Weekend,* was no different. The moral was that it's dangerous to drink. It was a moral we could take some comfort in.

Andy maneuvered to get next to me, and about halfway through the show he leaned a little closer and asked if I could get him Rita Hayworth. I'll tell you the truth, it kind of tickled me. He was usually cool, calm, and collected, but that night he was jumpy as hell, almost embarrassed, as if he was asking me to get him a load of Trojans or one of those sheepskin-lined gadgets that are supposed to "enhance your solitary pleasure," as the magazines put it. He seemed overcharged, a man on the verge of blowing his radiator.

"I can get her," I said. "No sweat, calm down. You want the big one or the little one?" At that time Rita was my best girl (a few years before it had been Betty Grable) and she came in two sizes. For a buck you could get the little Rita. For two-fifty you could have the big Rita, four feet high and all woman.

"The big one," he said, not looking at me. I tell you, he was a hot sketch that night. He was blushing just like a kid trying to get into a kootch show with his big brother's draftcard. "Can you do it?"

"Take it easy, sure I can. Does a bear shit in the woods?" The audience was applauding and catcalling as the bugs came out of the walls to get Ray Milland, who was having a bad case of the DT's.

"How soon?"

"A week. Maybe less."

"Okay." But he sounded disappointed, as if he had been hoping I had one stuffed down my pants right then. "How much?"

I quoted him the wholesale price. I could afford to give him this one at cost; he'd been a good customer, what with his rock-hammer and his rock-blankets. Furthermore, he'd been a good boy—on more than one night when he was having his problems with Bogs, Rooster, and the rest, I wondered how long it would be before he used the rock-hammer to crack someone's head open.

Posters are a big part of my business, just behind the booze and cigarettes, usually half a step ahead of the reefer. In the sixties the business exploded in every direction, with a lot of people wanting funky hang-ups like Jimi Hendrix, Bob Dylan, that *Easy Rider* poster. But mostly it's girls; one pin-up queen after another.

A few days after Andy spoke to me, a laundry driver I did business with back then brought in better than sixty posters, most of them Rita Hayworths. You may even remember the picture; I sure do. Rita is dressed—sort of—in a bathing suit, one hand behind her head, her eyes half-closed, those full, sulky red lips parted. They called it Rita Hayworth, but they might as well have called it Woman in Heat.

The prison administration knows about the black market, in case you were wondering. Sure they do. They probably know almost as much about my business as I do myself. They live with it because they know that a prison is like a big pressure-cooker, and there have to be vents somewhere to let off some steam. They make the occasional bust, and I've done time in solitary a time or three over the years, but when it's something like posters, they wink. Live and let live. And when a big Rita Hayworth went up in some fishie's cell, the assumption was that it came in the mail from a friend or a relative. Of course all the care-packages from friends and relatives are opened and the contents inventoried, but who goes back and re-checks the inventory sheets for something as harmless as a Rita Hayworth or an Ava Gardner pin-up? When you're in a pressure-cooker you learn to live and let live or somebody will carve you a brand-new mouth just above the Adam's apple. You learn to make allowances.

It was Ernie again who took the poster up to Andy's cell, 14, from my own, 6. And it was Ernie who brought back the note, written in Andy's careful hand, just one word: "Thanks."

A little while later, as they filed us out for morning chow, I glanced into his cell and saw Rita over his bunk in all her swimsuited glory, one hand behind her head, her eyes half-closed, those soft, satiny lips parted. It was over his bunk where he could look at her nights, after lights-out, in the glow of the arc sodiums in the exercise yard.

But in the bright morning sunlight, there were dark slashes across her face—the shadow of the bars on his single slit window.

Now I'm going to tell you what happened in mid-May of 1950 that finally ended Andy's three-year series of skirmishes with the sisters. It was also the incident which eventually got him out of the laundry and into the library, where he filled out his work-time until he left our happy little family earlier this year.

You may have noticed how much of what I've told you already is hearsay—someone saw something and told me and I told you. Well, in some cases I've simplified it even more than it really was, and have repeated (or will repeat) fourth- or fifth-hand information. That's the way it is here. The grapevine is very real, and you have to use it if you're going to stay ahead. Also, of course, you have to know how to pick out the grains of truth from the chaff of lies, rumors, and wish-it-had-beens.

You may also have gotten the idea that I'm describing some-one who's more legend than man, and I would have to agree that there's some truth to that. To us long-timers who knew Andy over a space of years, there was an element of fantasy to him, a sense, almost, of myth-magic, if you get what I mean. That story I passed on about Andy refusing to give Bogs Diamond a head-job is part of that myth, and how he kept on fighting the sisters is part of it, and how he got the library job is part of it, too . . . but with one important difference: I was there and I saw what happened, and I swear on my mother's name that it's all true. The oath of a convicted murderer may not be worth much, but believe this: I don't lie.

Andy and I were on fair speaking terms by then. The guy fascinated me. Looking back to the poster episode, I see there's one thing I neglected to tell you, and maybe I should. Five weeks after he hung Rita up (I'd forgotten all about it by then, and had gone on to other deals), Ernie passed a small white box through the bars of my cell.

"From Dufresne," he said, low, and never missed a stroke with his push-broom.

"Thanks, Ernie," I said, and slipped him half a pack of Camels.

Now what the hell was this, I was wondering as I slipped the cover from the box. There was a lot of white cotton inside, and below that . . .

I looked for a long time. For a few minutes it was like I didn't even dare touch them, they were so pretty. There's a crying shortage of pretty things in the slam, and the real pity of it is that a lot of men don't even seem to miss them.

There were two pieces of quartz in that box, both of them carefully polished. They had been chipped into driftwood shapes. There were little sparkles of iron pyrites in them like flecks of gold. If they hadn't been so heavy, they would have served as a fine pair of men's cufflinks—they were that close to being a matched set.

How much work went into creating those two pieces? Hours and hours after lights-out, I knew that. First the chipping and shaping, and then the almost endless polishing and finishing with those rock-blankets. Looking at them, I felt the warmth that any man or woman feels when he or she is looking at something pretty, something that has been *worked* and *made*—that's the thing that really separates us from the animals, I think—and I felt something else, too. A sense of awe for the man's brute persistence. But I never knew just how persistent Andy Dufresne could be until much later.

In May of 1950, the powers that be decided that the roof of the license-plate factory ought to be re-surfaced with roofing tar. They wanted it done before it got too hot up there, and they asked for volunteers for the work, which was planned to take about a week. More than seventy men spoke up, because it was outside work and May is one damn fine month for outside work. Nine or ten names were drawn out of a hat, and two of them happened to be Andy's and my own.

For the next week we'd be marched out to the exercise yard after breakfast, with two guards up front and two more behind . . . plus all the guards in the towers keeping a weather eye on the proceedings through their field-glasses for good measure.

Four of us would be carrying a big extension ladder on those morning marches—I always got a kick out of the way Dickie Betts, who was on that job, called that sort of ladder an extensible—and we'd put it up against the side of that low, flat building. Then we'd start bucket-brigading hot buckets of tar up to the roof. Spill that shit on you and you'd jitterbug all the way to the infirmary.

There were six guards on the project, all of them picked on the basis of seniority. It was almost as good as a week's vacation, because instead of sweating it out in the laundry or the plate-shop or standing over a bunch of cons cutting pulp or brush somewhere out in the willywags, they were having a regular May holiday in the sun, just sitting there with their backs up against the low parapet, shooting the bull back and forth.

They didn't even have to keep more than half an eye on us, because the south wall sentry post was close enough so that the fellows up there could have spit their chews on us, if they'd wanted to. If anyone on the roof-sealing party had made one funny move, it would take four seconds to cut him smack in two with .45-caliber machine-gun bullets. So those screws just sat there and took their ease. All they needed was a couple of six-packs buried in crushed ice, and they would have been the lords of all creation.

One of them was a fellow named Byron Hadley, and in that year of 1950, he'd been at Shawshank longer than I had. Longer than the last two wardens put together, as a matter of fact. The fellow running the show in 1950 was a prissy-looking downeast Yankee named George Dunahy. He had a degree in penal administration. No one liked him, as far as I could tell, except the people who had gotten him his appointment. I heard that he was only interested in three things: compiling statistics for a book (which was later published by a small New England outfit called Light Side Press, where he probably had to pay to have it done), which team won the intramural baseball championship each September, and getting a death-penalty law passed in Maine. A regular bear for the death-penalty was George Dunahy. He was fired off the job in 1953, when it came out he was running a discount auto-repair service down in the prison garage and splitting the profits with Byron Hadley and Greg Stammas. Hadley and Stammas came out of that one okay—they were old hands at keeping their asses covered—but Dunahy took a walk. No one was sorry to see him go, but nobody was exactly pleased to see Greg Stammas step into his shoes, either. He was a short man with a tight, hard gut and the coldest brown eyes you ever saw. He always had a painful, pursed little grin on his face, as if he had to go to the bathroom and couldn't quite manage it. During Stammas's tenure as warden there was a lot of brutality at Shawshank, and although I have no proof, I believe there were maybe half a dozen moonlight burials in the stand of scrub forest that lies east of the prison. Dunahy was bad, but Greg Stammas was a cruel, wretched, cold-hearted man.

He and Byron Hadley were good friends. As warden, George Dunahy was nothing but a posturing figurehead; it was Stammas, and through him, Hadley, who actually administered the prison.

Hadley was a tall, shambling man with thinning red hair. He sunburned easily and he talked loud and if you didn't move fast enough to suit him, he'd clout you with his stick. On that day, our third on the roof, he was talking to another guard named Mert Entwhistle.

Hadley had gotten some amazingly good news, so he was griping about it. That was his style—he was a thankless man with not a good word for anyone, a man who was convinced that the whole world was against him. The world had cheated him out of the best years of his life, and the world would be more than happy to cheat him out of the rest. I have seen some screws that I thought were almost saintly, and I think I know why that happens—they are able to see the difference between their own lives, poor and struggling as they might be, and the lives of the men they are paid by the State to watch over. These guards are able to formulate a comparison concerning pain. Others can't, or won't.

For Byron Hadley there was no basis of comparison. He could sit there, cool and at his ease under the warm May sun, and find the gall to mourn his own good luck while less than ten feet away a bunch of men were working and sweating and burning their hands on great big buckets filled with bubbling tar, men who had to work so hard in their ordinary round of days that this looked like a *respite.* You may remember the old question, the one that's supposed to define your outlook on life when you answer it. For Byron Hadley the answer would always be *half empty, the glass is half empty.* Forever and ever, amen. If you gave him a cool drink of apple cider, he'd think about vinegar. If you told him his wife had always been faithful to him, he'd tell you it was because she was so damn ugly.

So there he sat, talking to Mert Entwhistle loud enough for all of us to hear, his broad white forehead already starting to redden with the sun. He had one hand thrown back over the low parapet surrounding the roof. The other was on the butt of his .38.

We all got the story along with Mert. It seemed that Hadley's older brother had gone off to Texas some fourteen years ago and the rest of the family hadn't heard from the son of a bitch since. They had all assumed he was dead, and good riddance. Then, a week and a half ago, a lawyer had called them long-distance from Austin. It seemed that Hadley's brother had died four months ago, and a rich man at that ("It's frigging incredible how lucky some assholes can get," this paragon of gratitude on the plate-shop roof said). The money had come as a result of oil and oil-leases, and there was close to a million dollars.

No, Hadley wasn't a millionaire—that might have made even him happy, at least for awhile—but the brother had left a pretty damned decent bequest of thirty-five thousand dollars to each surviving member of his family back in Maine, if they could be found. Not bad. Like getting lucky and winning a sweepstakes.

But to Byron Hadley the glass was always half empty. He spent most of the morning bitching to Mert about the bite that the goddam government was going to take out of his windfall. "They'll leave me about enough to buy a new car with," he allowed, "and then what happens? You have to pay the damn taxes on the car, and the repairs and maintenance, you got your goddam kids pestering you to take 'em for a ride with the top down—"

"And to *drive* it, if they're old enough," Mert said. Old Mert Entwhistle knew which side his bread was buttered on, and he didn't say what must have been as obvious to him as to the rest of us: If that money's worrying you so bad, Byron old kid old sock, I'll just take it off your hands. After all, what are friends for?

"That's right, wanting to drive it, wanting to *learn* to drive on it, for Chrissake," Byron said with a shudder. "Then what happens at the end of the year? If you figured the tax wrong and you don't have enough left over to pay the overdraft, you got to pay out of your own pocket, or maybe even borrow it from one of those kikey loan agencies. And they audit you anyway, you know. It don't matter. And when the government audits you, they always take more. Who can fight Uncle Sam? He puts his hand inside your shirt and squeezes your tit until it's purple, and you end up getting the short end. Christ."

He lapsed into a morose silence, thinking of what terrible bad luck he'd had to inherit that thirty-five thousand dollars. Andy Dufresne had been spreading tar with a big Padd brush less than fifteen feet away and now he tossed it into his pail and walked over to where Mert and Hadley were sitting.

We all tightened up, and I saw one of the other screws, Tim Youngblood, drag his hand down to where his pistol was holstered. One of the fellows in the sentry tower struck his partner on the arm and they both turned, too. For one moment I thought Andy was going to get shot, or clubbed, or both.

Then he said, very softly, to Hadley: "Do you trust your wife?"

Hadley just stared at him. He was starting to get red in the face, and I knew that was a bad sign. In about three seconds he was going to pull his billy and give Andy the butt end of it right in the solar plexus, where that big bundle of nerves is. A hard enough hit there can kill you, but they always go for it. If it doesn't kill you it will paralyze you long enough to forget whatever cute move it was that you had planned.

"Boy," Hadley said, "I'll give you just one chance to pick up that Padd. And then you're goin off this roof on your head."

Andy just looked at him, very calm and still. His eyes were like ice. It was as if he hadn't heard. And I found myself wanting to tell him how it was, to give him the crash course. The crash course is you *never* let on that you hear the guards talking, you *never* try to horn in on their conversation unless you're asked (and then you always tell them just what they want to hear and shut up again). Black man, white man, red man, yellow man, in prison it doesn't matter because we've got our own brand of equality. In prison every con's a nigger and you have to get used to the idea if you intend to survive men like Hadley and Greg Stammas, who really would kill you just as soon as look at you. When you're in stir you belong to the State and if you forget it, woe is you. I've known men who've lost eyes, men who've lost toes and fingers; I knew one man who lost the tip of his penis and counted himself lucky that was all he lost. I wanted to tell Andy that it was already too late. He could go back and pick up his brush and there would still be some big lug waiting for him in the showers that night, ready to charley-horse both of his legs and leave him writhing on the cement. You could buy a lug like that for a pack of cigarettes or three Baby Ruths. Most of all, I wanted to tell him not to make it any worse than it already was.

What I did was to keep on running tar out onto the roof as if nothing at all was happening. Like everyone else, I look after my own ass first. I have to. It's cracked already, and in Shawshank there have always been Hadleys willing to finish the job of breaking it.

Andy said, "Maybe I put it wrong. Whether you trust her or not is immaterial. The problem is whether or not you believe she would ever go behind your back, try to hamstring you."

Hadley got up. Mert got up. Tim Youngblood got up. Hadley's face was as red as the side of a firebarn. "Your only problem," he said, "is going to be how many bones you still got unbroken. You can count them in the infirmary. Come on, Mert. We're throwing this sucker over the side."

Tim Youngblood drew his gun. The rest of us kept tarring like mad. The sun beat down. They were going to do it; Hadley

and Mert were simply going to pitch him over the side. Terrible accident. Dufresne, prisoner 81433-SHNK, was taking
a couple of empties down and slipped on the ladder. Too bad.

They laid hold of him, Mert on the right arm, Hadley on
the left. Andy didn't resist. His eyes never left Hadley's red,
horsey face.

"If you've got your thumb on her, Mr. Hadley," he said in
that same calm, composed voice, "there's not a reason why you
shouldn't have every cent of that money. Final score, Mr. Byron
Hadley thirty-five thousand, Uncle Sam zip."

Mert started to drag him toward the edge. Hadley just stood
there. For a moment Andy was like a rope between them in
a tug-of-war game. Then Hadley said, "Hold on one second,
Mert. What do you mean, boy?"

"I mean, if you've got your thumb on your wife, you can
give it to her," Andy said.

"You better start making sense, boy, or you're going over."

"The IRS allows you a one-time-only gift to your spouse,"
Andy said. "It's good up to sixty thousand dollars."

Hadley was now looking at Andy as if he had been pole-
axed. "Naw, that ain't right," he said. "Tax *free?*"

"Tax free," Andy said. "IRS can't touch one cent."

"How would you know a thing like that?"

Tim Youngblood said: "He used to be a banker, Byron. I
s'pose he might—"

"Shut ya head, Trout," Hadley said without looking at him.
Tim Youngblood flushed and shut up. Some of the guards
called him Trout because of his thick lips and buggy eyes.
Hadley kept looking at Andy. "You're the smart banker who
shot his wife. Why should I believe a smart banker like you?
So I can wind up in here breaking rocks right alongside you?
You'd like that, wouldn't you?"

Andy said quietly: "If you went to jail for tax evasion, you'd
go to a federal penitentiary, not Shawshank. But you won't.
The tax-free gift to the spouse is a perfectly legal loophole. I've

done dozens . . . no, hundreds of them. It's meant primarily for people with small businesses to pass on, for people who come into one-time-only windfalls. Like yourself."

"I think you're lying," Hadley said, but he didn't—you could see he didn't. There was an emotion dawning on his face, something that was grotesque overlying that long, ugly countenance and that receding, sunburned brow. An almost obscene emotion when seen on the features of Byron Hadley. It was hope.

"No, I'm not lying. There's no reason why you should take my word for it, either. Engage a lawyer—"

"Ambulance-chasing highway-robbing cocksuckers!" Hadley cried.

Andy shrugged. "Then go to the IRS. They'll tell you the same thing for free. Actually, you don't need me to tell you at all. You would have investigated the matter for yourself."

"You're fucking-A. I don't need any smart wife-killing banker to show me where the bear shit in the buckwheat."

"You'll need a tax lawyer or a banker to set up the gift for you and that will cost you something," Andy said. "Or . . . if you were interested, I'd be glad to set it up for you nearly free of charge. The price would be three beers apiece for my co-workers—"

"Co-workers," Mert said, and let out a rusty guffaw. He slapped his knee. A real knee-slapper was old Mert, and I hope he died of intestinal cancer in a part of the world where morphine is as of yet undiscovered. "Co-workers, ain't that cute? Co-workers? You ain't got any—"

"Shut your friggin trap," Hadley growled, and Mert shut. Hadley looked at Andy again. "What was you sayin?"

"I was saying that I'd only ask three beers apiece for my co-workers, if that seems fair," Andy said. "I think a man feels more like a man when he's working out of doors in the spring-time if he can have a bottle of suds. That's only my opinion. It would go down smooth, and I'm sure you'd have their gratitude."

I have talked to some of the other men who were up there that day—Rennie Martin, Logan St. Pierre, and Paul Bonsaint were three of them—and we all saw the same thing then . . . *felt* the same thing. Suddenly it was Andy who had the upper hand. It was Hadley who had the gun on his hip and the billy in his hand, Hadley who had his friend Greg Stammas behind him and the whole prison administration behind Stammas, the whole power of the State behind *that,* but all at once in that golden sunshine it didn't matter, and I felt my heart leap up in my chest as it never had since the truck drove me and four others through the gate back in 1938 and I stepped out into the exercise yard.

Andy was looking at Hadley with those cold, clear, calm eyes, and it wasn't just the thirty-five thousand then, we all agreed on that. I've played it over and over in my mind and I *know.* It was man against man, and Andy simply *forced* him, the way a strong man can force a weaker man's wrist to the table in a game of Indian rasseling. There was no reason, you see, why Hadley couldn't've given Mert the nod at that very minute, pitched Andy overside onto his head, and still taken Andy's advice.

No reason. *But he didn't.*

"I could get you all a couple of beers if I wanted to," Hadley said. "A beer does taste good while you're workin." The colossal prick even managed to sound magnanimous.

"I'd just give you one piece of advice the IRS wouldn't bother with," Andy said. His eyes were fixed unwinkingly on Hadley's. "Make this gift to your wife if you're *sure.* If you think there's even a chance she might double-cross you or backshoot you, we could work out something else—"

"Double-cross me?" Hadley asked harshly. "Double-cross *me?* Mr. Hotshot Banker, if she ate her way through a boxcar of Ex-Lax, she wouldn't dare fart unless I gave her the nod."

Mert, Youngblood, and the other screws yucked it up dutifully. Andy never cracked a smile.

"I'll write down the forms you need," he said. "You can get them at the post office, and I'll fill them out for your signature."

That sounded suitably important, and Hadley's chest swelled. Then he glared around at the rest of us and hollered, "What are you jimmies starin at? Move your asses, goddammit!" He looked back at Andy. "You come over here with me, hotshot. And listen to me well: if you're jewing me somehow, you're gonna find yourself chasing your own head around Shower C before the week's out."

"Yes, I understand that," Andy said softly.

And he did understand it. The way it turned out, he understood a lot more than I did—more than any of us did.

That's how, on the second-to-last day of the job, the convict crew that tarred the plate-factory roof in 1950 ended up sitting in a row at ten o'clock on a spring morning, drinking Black Label beer supplied by the hardest screw that ever walked a turn at Shawshank State Prison. That beer was piss-warm, but it was still the best I ever had in my life. We sat and drank it and felt the sun on our shoulders, and not even the expression of half-amusement, half-contempt on Hadley's face—as if he were watching apes drink beer instead of men—could spoil it. It lasted twenty minutes, that beer-break, and for those twenty minutes we felt like free men. We could have been drinking beer and tarring the roof of one of our own houses.

Only Andy didn't drink. I already told you about his drinking habit. He sat hunkered down in the shade, hands dangling between his knees, watching us and smiling a little. It's amazing how many men remember him that way, and amazing how many men were on that work-crew when Andy Dufresne faced down Byron Hadley. I thought there were nine or ten of us, but by 1955 there must have been two hundred of us, maybe more . . . if you believed what you heard.

So yeah—if you asked me to give you a flat-out answer to the question of whether I'm trying to tell you about a man or a legend that got made up around the man, like a pearl around a little piece of grit—I'd have to say that the answer lies somewhere in between. All I know for sure is that Andy Dufresne wasn't much like me or anyone else I ever knew since I came inside. He brought in five hundred dollars jammed up his back porch, but somehow that graymeat son of a bitch managed to bring in something else as well. A sense of his own worth, maybe, or a feeling that he would be the winner in the end . . . or maybe it was only a sense of freedom, even inside these goddamned gray walls. It was a kind of inner light he carried around with him. I only knew him to lose that light once, and that is also a part of this story.

By World Series time of 1950—this was the year the Philadelphia Whiz Kids dropped four straight, you will remember—Andy was having no more trouble from the sisters. Stammas and Hadley had passed the word. If Andy Dufresne came to either of them, or any of the other screws that formed a part of their coterie, and showed so much as a single drop of blood in his underpants, every sister in Shawshank would go to bed that night with a headache. They didn't fight it. As I have pointed out, there was always an eighteen-year-old car thief or a firebug or some guy who'd gotten his kicks handling little children. After the day on the plate-shop roof, Andy went his way and the sisters went theirs.

He was working in the library then, under a tough old con named Brooks Hatlen. Hatlen had gotten the job back in the late twenties because he had a college education. Brooksie's degree was in animal husbandry, true enough, but college educations in institutes of lower learning like The Shank are so rare that it's a case of beggars not being able to be choosers.

In 1952 Brooksie, who had killed his wife and daughter after a losing streak at poker back when Coolidge was President, was paroled. As usual, the State in all its wisdom had let him go long after any chance he might have had to become a useful part of society was gone. He was sixty-eight and arthritic when he tottered out of the main gate in his Polish suit and his French shoes, his parole papers in one hand and a Greyhound bus ticket in the other. He was crying when he left. Shawshank was his world. What lay beyond its walls was as terrible to Brooks as the Western Seas had been to superstitious fifteenth-century sailors. In prison, Brooksie had been a person of some importance. He was the librarian, an educated man. If he went to the Kittery library and asked for a job, they wouldn't even give him a library card. I heard he died in a home for indigent old folks up Freeport way in 1953, and at that he lasted about six months longer than I thought he would. Yeah, I guess the State got its own back on Brooksie, all right. They trained him to like it inside the shithouse and then they threw him out.

Andy succeeded to Brooksie's job, and he was librarian for twenty-three years. He used the same force of will I'd seen him use on Byron Hadley to get what he wanted for the library, and I saw him gradually turn one small room (which still smelled of turpentine because it had been a paint closet until 1922 and had never been properly aired) lined with Reader's Digest Condensed Books and *National Geographies* into the best prison library in New England.

He did it a step at a time. He put a suggestion box by the door and patiently weeded out such attempts at humor as *More Fuk-Boox Pleeze* and *Excape in 10 EZ Lesions.* He got hold of the things the prisoners seemed serious about. He wrote to the major book clubs in New York and got two of them, The Literary Guild and The Book-of-the-Month Club, to send editions of all their major selections to us at a special cheap rate. He discovered a hunger for information on such small hobbies as soap-carving, woodworking, sleight of hand, and card solitaire. He got all the books he could on such subjects. And those two jailhouse staples, Erie Stanley Gardner and Louis L' Amour. Cons never seem to get enough of the courtroom or the open range. And yes, he did keep a box of fairly spicy paperbacks under the checkout desk, loaning them out carefully and making sure they always got back. Even so, each new acquisition of that type was quickly read to tatters.

He began to write to the State Senate in Augusta in 1954. Stammas was warden by then, and he used to pretend Andy was some sort of mascot. He was always in the library, shooting the bull with Andy, and sometimes he'd even throw a paternal arm around Andy's shoulders or give him a goose. He didn't fool anybody. Andy Dufresne was no one's mascot.

He told Andy that maybe he'd been a banker on the outside, but that part of his life was receding rapidly into his past and he had better get a hold on the facts of prison life. As far as that bunch of jumped-up Republican Rotarians in Augusta was concerned, there were only three viable expenditures of the taxpayers' money in the field of prisons and corrections. Number one was more walls, number two was more bars, and number three was more guards. As far as the State Senate was concerned, Stammas explained, the folks in Thomaston and Shawshank and Pittsfield and South Portland were the scum of the earth. They were there to do hard time, and by God and Sonny Jesus, it was hard time they were going to do. And if there were a few weevils in the bread, wasn't that just too fucking bad?

Andy smiled his small, composed smile and asked Stammas what would happen to a block of concrete if a drop of water fell on it once every year for a million years. Stammas laughed and clapped Andy on the back. "You got no million years, old horse, but if you did, I bleeve you'd do it with that same little grin on your face. You go on and write your letters. I'll even mail them for you if you pay for the stamps."

Which Andy did. And he had the last laugh, although Stammas and Hadley weren't around to see it. Andy's requests for library funds were routinely turned down until 1960, when he received a check for two hundred dollars—the Senate probably appropriated it in hopes that he would shut up and go away. Vain hope. Andy felt that he had finally gotten one foot in the door and he simply redoubled his efforts; two letters a week instead of one. In 1962 he got four hundred dollars, and for the rest of the decade the library received seven hundred dollars a year like clockwork. By 1971 that had risen to an even thousand. Not much stacked up against what your average small-town library receives, I guess, but a thousand bucks can buy a lot of recycled Perry Mason stories and Jake Logan Westerns. By the time Andy left, you could go into the library (expanded from its original paint-locker to three rooms), and find just about anything you'd want. And if you couldn't find it, chances were good that Andy could get it for you.

Now you're asking yourself if all this came about just because Andy told Byron Hadley how to save the taxes on his windfall inheritance. The answer is yes . . . and no. You can probably figure out what happened for yourself.

Word got around that Shawshank was housing its very own pet financial wizard. In the late spring and the summer of 1950, Andy set up two trust funds for guards who wanted to assure a college education for their kids, he advised a couple of others who wanted to take small fliers in common stock (and they did pretty damn well, as things turned out; one of them did so well he was able to take an early retirement two years later), and I'll be damned if he didn't advise the warden himself, old Lemon Lips George Dunahy, on how to go about setting up a tax-shelter for himself. That was just before Dunahy got the bum's rush, and I believe he must have been dreaming about all the millions his book was going to make him. By April of 1951, Andy was doing the tax returns for half the screws at Shawshank, and by 1952, he was doing almost all of them. He was paid in what may be a prison's most valuable coin: simple good will.

Later on, after Greg Stammas took over the warden's office, Andy became even more important—but if I tried to tell you the specifics of just how, I'd be guessing. There are some things I know about and others I can only guess at. I know that there were some prisoners who received all sorts of special considerations—radios in their cells, extraordinary visiting privileges, things like that—and there were people on the outside who were paying for them to have those privileges. Such people are known as "angels" by the prisoners. All at once some fellow would be excused from working in the plate-shop on Saturday forenoons, and you'd know that fellow had an angel out there who'd coughed up a chunk of dough to make sure it happened. The way it usually works is that the angel will pay the bribe to some middle-level screw, and the screw will spread the grease both up and down the administrative ladder.

Then there was the discount auto-repair service that laid Warden Dunahy low. It went underground for awhile and then emerged stronger than ever in the late fifties. And some of the contractors that worked at the prison from time to time were paying kickbacks to the top administration officials, I'm pretty sure, and the same was almost certainly true of the companies whose equipment was bought and installed in the laundry and the license-plate shop and the stamping-mill that was built in 1963.

By the late sixties there was also a booming trade in pills, and the same administrative crowd was involved in turning a buck on that. All of it added up to a pretty good-sized river of illicit income. Not like the pile of clandestine bucks that must fly around a really big prison like Attica or San Quentin, but not peanuts, either. And money itself becomes a problem after awhile. You can't just stuff it into your wallet and then shell out a bunch of crumpled twenties and dog-eared tens when you want a pool built in your back yard or an addition put on your house. Once you get past a certain point, you have to explain where that money came from . . . and if your explanations aren't convincing enough, you're apt to wind up wearing a number yourself.

So there was a need for Andy's services. They took him out of the laundry and installed him in the library, but if you wanted to look at it another away, they never took him out of the laundry at all. They just set him to work washing dirty money instead of dirty sheets. He funnelled it into stocks, bonds, tax-free municipals, you name it.

He told me once about ten years after that day on the plate-shop roof that his feelings about what he was doing were pretty clear, and that his conscience was relatively untroubled. The rackets would have gone on with him or without him. He had not asked to be sent to Shawshank, he went on; he was an inno-cent man who had been victimized by colossal bad luck, not a missionary or a do-gooder.

"Besides, Red," he told me with that same half-grin, "what I'm doing in here isn't all *that* different from what I was doing outside. I'll hand you a pretty cynical axiom: the amount of expert financial help an individual or company needs rises in direct proportion to how many people that person or business is screwing.

"The people who run this place are stupid, brutal monsters for the most part. The people who run the straight world are brutal and monstrous, but they happen not to be quite as stu-pid, because the standard of competence out there is a little higher. Not much, but a little."

"But the pills," I said. "I don't want to tell you your busi-ness, but they make me nervous. Reds, uppers, downers, Nem-butals—now they've got these things they call Phase Fours. I won't get anything like that. Never have."

"No," Andy said. "I don't like the pills, either. Never have. But I'm not much of a one for cigarettes or booze, either. But I don't push the pills. I don't bring them in, and I don't sell them once they are in. Mostly it's the screws who do that."

"But—"

"Yeah, I know. There's a fine line there. What it comes down to, Red, is some people refuse to get their hands dirty at all.

That's called sainthood, and the pigeons land on your shoulders and crap all over your shirt. The other extreme is to take a bath in the dirt and deal any goddamned thing that will turn a dollar—guns, switchblades, big H, what the hell. You ever have a con come up to you and offer you a contract?"

I nodded. It's happened a lot of times over the years. You are, after all, the man who can get it. And they figure if you can get them batteries for their transistor radios or cartons of Luckies or lids of reefer, you can put them in touch with a guy who'll use a knife.

"Sure you have," Andy agreed. "But you don't do it. Because guys like us, Red, we know there's a third choice. An alternative to staying simon-pure or bathing in the filth and the slime. It's the alternative that grown-ups all over the world pick. You balance off your walk through the hog-wallow against what it gains you. You choose the lesser of two evils and try to keep your good intentions in front of you. And I guess you judge how well you're doing by how well you sleep at night . . . and what your dreams are like."

"Good intentions," I said, and laughed. "I know all about that, Andy. A fellow can toddle right off to hell on that road."

"Don't you believe it," he said, growing somber. "This is hell right here. Right here in The Shank. They sell pills and I tell them what to do with the money. But I've also got the library, and I know of over two dozen guys who have used the books in there to help them pass their high school equivalency tests. Maybe when they get out of here they'll be able to crawl off the shitheap. When we needed that second room back in 1957, I got it. Because they want to keep me happy. I work cheap. That's the trade-off."

"And you've got your own private quarters."

"Sure. That's the way I like it."

The prison population had risen slowly all through the fifties, and it damn near exploded in the sixties, what with every college-kid in America wanting to try dope and the perfectly ridiculous penalties for the use of a little reefer. But in all that time Andy never had a cellmate, except for a big, silent Indian named Normaden (like all Indians in The Shank, he was called Chief), and Normaden didn't last long. A lot of the other long-timers thought Andy was crazy, but Andy just smiled. He lived alone and he liked it that way . . . and as he'd said, they liked to keep him happy. He worked cheap.

Prison time is slow time, sometimes you'd swear it's stop-time, but it passes. It passes. George Dunahy departed the scene in a welter of newspaper headlines shouting scandal and nest-feathering. Stammas succeeded him, and for the next six years Shawshank was a kind of living hell. During the reign of Greg Stammas, the beds in the infirmary and the cells in the Solitary Wing were always full.

One day in 1958 I looked at myself in a small shaving mirror I kept in my cell and saw a forty-year-old man looking back at me. A kid had come in back in 1938, a kid with a big mop of carroty red hair, half-crazy with remorse, thinking about suicide. That kid was gone. The red hair was going gray and starting to recede. There were crow's tracks around the eyes. On that day I could see an old man inside, waiting his time to come out. It scared me. Nobody wants to grow old in stir.

Stammas went early in 1959. There had been several investigative reporters sniffing around, and one of them even did four months under an assumed name, for a crime made up out of whole cloth. They were getting ready to drag out scandal and nest-feathering again, but before they could bring the hammer down on him, Stammas ran. I can understand that; boy, can I ever. If he had been tried and convicted, he could have ended up right in here. If so, he might have lasted all of five hours. Byron Hadley had gone two years earlier. The sucker had a heart attack and took an early retirement.

Andy never got touched by the Stammas affair. In early 1959 a new warden was appointed, and a new assistant warden, and a new chief of guards. For the next eight months or so, Andy was just another con again. It was during that period that Normaden, the big half-breed Passamaquoddy, shared Andy's cell with him. Then everything just started up again. Normaden was moved out, and Andy was living in solitary splendor again. The names at the top change, but the rackets never do.

I talked to Normaden once about Andy. "Nice fella," Normaden said. It was hard to make out anything he said because he had a harelip and a cleft palate; his words all came out in a slush. "I liked it there. He never made fun. But he didn't want me there. I could tell." Big shrug. "I was glad to go, me. Bad draft in that cell. All the time cold. He don't let nobody touch his things. That's okay. Nice man, never made fun. But big draft."

Rita Hayworth hung in Andy's cell until 1955, if I remember right. Then it was Marilyn Monroe, that picture from *The Seven-Year Itch* where she's standing over a subway grating and the warm air is flipping her skirt up. Marilyn lasted until 1960, and she was considerably tattered about the edges when Andy replaced her with Jayne Mansfield. Jayne was, you should pardon the expression, a bust. After only a year or so she was replaced with an English actress—might have been Hazel Court, but I'm not sure. In 1966 that one came down and Raquel Welch went up for a record-breaking six-year engagement in Andy's cell. The last poster to hang there was a pretty country-rock singer whose name was Linda Ronstadt.

I asked him once what the posters meant to him, and he gave me a peculiar, surprised sort of look. "Why, they mean the same thing to me as they do to most cons, I guess," he said. "Freedom. You look at those pretty women and you feel like you could almost . . . not quite but *almost* . . . step right through and be beside them. Be free. I guess that's why I always liked Raquel Welch the best. It wasn't just her; it was that beach she was standing on. Looked like she was down in Mexico somewhere. Someplace quiet, where a man would be able to hear himself think. Didn't you ever feel that way about a picture, Red? That you could almost step right through it?"

I said I'd never really thought of it that way.

"Maybe someday you'll see what I mean," he said, and he was right. Years later I saw exactly what he meant . . . and when I did, the first thing I thought of was Normaden, and about how he'd said it was always cold in Andy's cell.

A terrible thing happened to Andy in late March or early April of 1963. I have told you that he had something that most of the other prisoners, myself included, seemed to lack. Call it a sense of equanimity, or a feeling of inner peace, maybe even a constant and unwavering faith that someday the long nightmare would end. Whatever you want to call it, Andy Dufresne always seemed to have his act together. There was none of that sullen desperation about him that seems to afflict most lifers after awhile; you could never smell hopelessness on him. Until that late winter of '63.

We had another warden by then, a man named Samuel Norton. The Mathers, Cotton and Increase, would have felt right at home with Sam Norton. So far as I know, no one had ever seen him so much as crack a smile. He had a thirty-year pin from the Baptist Advent Church of Eliot. His major innovation as the head of our happy family was to make sure that each incoming prisoner had a New Testament. He had a small plaque on his desk, gold letters inlaid in teakwood, which said CHRIST IS MY SAVIOR. A sampler on the wall, made by his wife, read: HIS JUDGMENT COMETH AND THAT RIGHT EARLY. This latter sentiment cut zero ice with most of us. We felt that the judgment had already occurred, and we would be willing to testify with the best of them that the rock would not hide us nor the dead tree give us shelter. He had a Bible quote for every occasion, did Mr. Sam Norton, and whenever you meet a man like that, my best advice to you would be to grin big and cover up your balls with both hands.

There were less infirmary cases than in the days of Greg Stammas, and so far as I know the moonlight burials ceased altogether, but this is not to say that Norton was not a believer in punishment. Solitary was always well populated. Men lost their teeth not from beatings but from bread and water diets. It began to be called grain and drain, as in "I'm on the Sam Norton grain and drain train, boys."

The man was the foulest hypocrite that I ever saw in a high position. The rackets I told you about earlier continued to flourish, but Sam Norton added his own new wrinkles. Andy knew about them all, and because we had gotten to be pretty good friends by that time, he let me in on some of them. When Andy talked about them, an expression of amused, disgusted wonder would come over his face, as if he were telling me about some ugly, predatory species of bug that was, by its very ugliness and greed, somehow more comic than terrible.

It was Warden Norton who instituted the "Inside-Out" program you may have read about some sixteen or seventeen years back; it was even written up in *Newsweek*. In the press it sounded like a real advance in practical corrections and reha- bilitation. There were prisoners out cutting pulpwood, pris- oners repairing bridges and causeways, prisoners constructing potato cellars. Norton called it "Inside-Out" and was invited to explain it to damn near every Rotary and Kiwanis club in New England, especially after he got his picture in *Newsweek*. The prisoners called it "road-ganging," but so far as I know, none of them were ever invited to express their views to the Kiwanians or the Loyal Order of Moose.

Norton was right in there on every operation, thirty-year church-pin and all; from cutting pulp to digging storm-drains to laying new culverts under state highways, there was Nor- ton, skimming off the top. There were a hundred ways to do it—men, materials, you name it. But he had it coming another

51

way, as well. The construction businesses in the area were deathly afraid of Norton's Inside-Out program, because prison labor is slave labor, and you can't compete with that. So Sam Norton, he of the Testaments and the thirty-year church-pin, was passed a good many thick envelopes under the table during his sixteen-year tenure as Shawshank's warden. And when an envelope was passed, he would either overbid the project, not bid at all, or claim that all his Inside-Outers were committed elsewhere. It has always been something of a wonder to me that Norton was never found in the trunk of a Thunderbird parked off a highway somewhere down in Massachusetts with his hands tied behind his back and half a dozen bullets in his head.

Anyway, as the old barrelhouse song says, My God, how the money rolled in. Norton must have subscribed to the old Puritan notion that the best way to figure out which folks God favors is by checking their bank accounts.

Andy Dufresne was his right hand in all of this, his silent partner. The prison library was Andy's hostage to fortune. Norton knew it, and Norton used it. Andy told me that one of Norton's favorite aphorisms was *One hand washes the other.* So Andy gave good advice and made useful suggestions. I can't say for sure that he hand-tooled Norton's Inside-Out program, but I'm damned sure he processed the money for the Jesus-shouting son of a whore. He gave good advice, made useful suggestions, the money got spread around, and . . . son of a bitch! The library would get a new set of automotive repair manuals, a fresh set of Grolier Encyclopedias, books on how to prepare for the Scholastic Achievement Tests. And, of course, more Erie Stanley Gardners and more Louis L'Amours.

And I'm convinced that what happened happened because Norton just didn't want to lose his good right hand. I'll go further: it happened because he was scared of what might happen—what Andy might say against him—if Andy ever got clear of Shawshank State Prison.

I got the story a chunk here and a chunk there over a space of seven years, some of it from Andy—but not all. He never wanted to talk about that part of his life, and I don't blame him. I got parts of it from maybe half a dozen different sources. I've said once that prisoners are nothing but slaves, but they have that slave habit of looking dumb and keeping their ears open. I got it backwards and forwards and in the middle, but I'll give it to you from point A to point Z, and maybe you'll understand why the man spent about ten months in a bleak, depressed daze. See, I don't think he knew the truth until 1963, fifteen years after he came into this sweet little hell-hole. Until he met Tommy Williams, I don't think he knew how bad it could get.

Tommy Williams joined our happy little Shawshank family in November of 1962. Tommy thought of himself as a native of Massachusetts, but he wasn't proud; in his twenty-seven years he'd done time all over New England. He was a professional thief, and as you may have guessed, my own feeling was that he should have picked another profession.

He was a married man, and his wife came to visit each and every week. She had an idea that things might go better with Tommy—and consequently better with their three-year-old son and herself—if he got his high school degree. She talked him into it, and so Tommy Williams started visiting the library on a regular basis.

For Andy, this was an old routine by then. He saw that Tommy got a series of high school equivalency tests. Tommy would brush up on the subjects he had passed in high school—there weren't many—and then take the test. Andy also saw that he was enrolled in a number of correspondence courses covering the subjects he had failed in school or just missed by dropping out.

He probably wasn't the best student Andy ever took over the jumps, and I don't know if he ever did get his high school diploma, but that forms no part of my story. The important thing was that he came to like Andy Dufresne very much, as most people did after awhile.

On a couple of occasions he asked Andy "what a smart guy like you is doing in the joint"—a question which is the rough equivalent of that one that goes "What's a nice girl like you doing in a place like this?" But Andy wasn't the type to tell him; he would only smile and turn the conversation into some other channel. Quite normally, Tommy asked someone else, and when he finally got the story, I guess he also got the shock of his young life.

The person he asked was his partner on the laundry's steam ironer and folder. The inmates call this device the mangler, because that's exactly what it will do to you if you aren't paying attention and get your bad self caught in it. His partner was Charlie Lathrop, who had been in for about twelve years on a murder charge. He was more than glad to reheat the details of the Dufresne murder trial for Tommy; it broke the monotony of pulling freshly pressed bedsheets out of the machine and tucking them into the basket. He was just getting to the jury waiting until after lunch to bring in their guilty verdict when the trouble whistle went off and the mangle grated to a stop. They had been feeding in freshly washed sheets from the Eliot Nursing Home at the far end; these were spat out dry and neatly pressed at Tommy's and Charlie's end at the rate of one every five seconds. Their job was to grab them, fold them, and slap them into the cart, which had already been lined with clean brown paper.

But Tommy Williams was just standing there, staring at Charlie Lathrop, his mouth unhinged all the way to his chest. He was standing in a drift of sheets that had come through clean and which were now sopping up all the wet muck on the floor—and in a laundry wetwash, there's plenty of muck.

So the head bull that day, Homer Jessup, comes rushing over, bellowing his head off and on the prod for trouble.

Tommy took no notice of him. He spoke to Charlie as if old Homer, who had busted more heads than he could probably count, hadn't been there.

"What did you say that golf pro's name was?"

"Quentin," Charlie answered back, all confused and upset by now. He later said that the kid was as white as a truce flag. "Glenn Quentin, I think. Something like that, anyway—"

"Here now, here now," Homer Jessup roared, his neck as red as a rooster's comb. "Get them sheets in cold water! Get quick! Get quick, by Jesus, you—"

"Glenn Quentin, oh my God," Tommy Williams said, and that was all he got to say because Homer Jessup, that least peaceable of men, brought his billy down behind his ear. Tommy hit the floor so hard he broke off three of his front teeth. When he woke up he was in solitary, and confined to same for a week, riding a boxcar on Sam Norton's famous grain and drain train. Plus a black mark on his report card.

That was in early February of 1963, and Tommy Williams went around to six or seven other long-timers after he got out of solitary and got pretty much the same story. I know; I was one of them. But when I asked him why he wanted it, he just clammed up.

Then one day he went to the library and spilled one helluva big budget of information to Andy Dufresne. And for the first and last time, at least since he had approached me about the Rita Hayworth poster like a kid buying his first pack of Trojans, Andy lost his cool . . . only this time he blew it entirely.

I saw him later that day, and he looked like a man who has stepped on the business end of a rake and given himself a good one, whap between the eyes. His hands were trembling, and when I spoke to him, he didn't answer. Before that afternoon was out he had caught up with Billy Hanlon, who was the head screw, and set up an appointment with Warden Norton for the following day. He told me later that he didn't sleep a wink all that night; he just listened to a cold winter wind howling outside, watched the searchlights go around and around, putting long, moving shadows on the cement walls of the cage he had called home since Harry Truman was President, and tried to think it all out. He said it was as if Tommy had produced a key which fit a cage in the back of his mind, a cage like his own cell. Only instead of holding a man, that cage held a tiger, and that tiger's name was Hope. Williams had produced the key that unlocked the cage and the tiger was out, willy-nilly, to roam his brain.

Four years before, Tommy Williams had been arrested in Rhode Island, driving a stolen car that was full of stolen merchandise. Tommy turned in his accomplice, the DA played ball, and he got a lighter sentence . . . two to four, with time served. Eleven months after beginning his term, his old cellmate got a ticket out and Tommy got a new one, a man named Elwood Blatch. Blatch had been busted for burglary with a weapon and was serving six to twelve.

"I never seen such a high-strung guy," Tommy told me. "A man like that should never want to be a burglar, specially not with a gun. The slightest little noise, he'd go three feet into the air . . . and come down shooting, more likely than not. One night he almost strangled me because some guy down the hall was whopping on his cell bars with a tin cup.

"I did seven months with him, until they let me walk free. I got time served and time off, you understand. I can't say we talked because you didn't, you know, exactly hold a conversation with El Blatch. *He* held a conversation with *you*. He talked all the time. Never shut up. If you tried to get a word in, he'd shake his fist at you and roll his eyes. It gave me the cold chills whenever he done that. Big tall guy he was, mostly bald, with these green eyes set way down deep in the sockets. Jeez, I hope I never see him again.

"It was like a talkin jag every night. Where he grew up, the orphanages he run away from, the jobs he done, the women he fucked, the crap games he cleaned out. I just let him run on. My face ain't much, but I didn't want it, you know, rearranged for me.

"According to him, he'd burgled over two hundred joints. It was hard for me to believe, a guy like him who went off like a firecracker every time someone cut a loud fart, but he swore it was true. Now . . . listen to me, Red. I know guys sometimes make things up after they know a thing, but even before I knew about this golf pro guy, Quentin, I remember thinking that if El Blatch ever burgled *my* house, and I found out about it later, I'd have to count myself just about the luckiest motherfucker going still to be alive. Can you imagine him in some lady's bedroom, sifting through her jool'ry box, and she coughs in her sleep or turns over quick? It gives me the cold chills just to think of something like that, I swear on my mother's name it does.

"He said he'd killed people, too. People that gave him shit. At least that's what he said. And I believed him. He sure looked like a man that could do some killing. He was just so fucking high-strung! Like a pistol with a sawed-off firing pin. I knew a guy who had a Smith and Wesson Police Special with a sawed-off firing pin. It wasn't no good for nothing, except maybe for something to jaw about. The pull on that gun was so light that it would fire if this guy, Johnny Callahan, his name was, if he turned his record-player on full volume and put it on top of one of the speakers. That's how El Blatch was. I can't explain it any better. I just never doubted that he had greased some people.

"So one night, just for something to say, I go: 'Who'd you kill?' Like a joke, you know. So he laughs and says: 'There's one guy doing time up-Maine for these two people I killed. It was this guy and the wife of the slob who's doing the time. I was creeping their place and the guy started to give me some shit.'

"I can't remember if he ever told me the woman's name or not," Tommy went on. "Maybe he did. But in New England, Dufresne's like Smith or Jones in the rest of the country, because there's so many Frogs up here. Dufresne, Lavesque, Ouelette, Poulin, who can remember Frog names? But he told me the guy's name. He said the guy was Glenn Quentin and he was a prick, a big rich prick, a golf pro. El said he thought the guy might have cash in the house, maybe as much as five thousand dollars. That was a lot of money back then, he says to me. So I go: 'When was that?' And he goes: 'After the war. Just after the war.'

"So he went in and he did the joint and they woke up and the guy gave him some trouble. That's what *El* said. Maybe the guy just started to snore, that's what *I* say. Anyway, El said Quentin was in the sack with some hotshot lawyer's wife and they sent the lawyer up to Shawshank State Prison. Then he laughs this big laugh. Holy Christ, I was never so glad of anything as I was when I got my walking papers from that place."

I guess you can see why Andy went a little wonky when Tommy told him that story, and why he wanted to see the warden right away. Elwood Blatch had been serving a six-to-twelve rap when Tommy knew him four years before. By the time Andy heard all of this, in 1963, he might be on the verge of getting out . . . or already out. So those were the two prongs of the spit Andy was roasting on—the idea that Blatch might still be in on one hand, and the very real possibility that he might be gone like the wind on the other.

There were inconsistencies in Tommy's story, but aren't there always in real life? Blatch told Tommy the man who got sent up was a hotshot lawyer, and Andy was a banker, but those are two professions that people who aren't very educated could easily get mixed up. And don't forget that twelve years had gone by between the time Blatch was reading the clippings about the trial and the time he told the tale to Tommy Williams. He also told Tommy he got better than a thousand dollars from a footlocker Quentin had in his closet, but the police said at Andy's trial that there had been no sign of burglary. I have a few ideas about that. First, if you take the cash and the man it belonged to is dead, how are you going to know anything was stolen, unless someone else can tell you it was there to start with? Second, who's to say Blatch wasn't lying about that part of it? Maybe he didn't want to admit killing two people for nothing. Third, maybe there were signs of burglary and the cops either overlooked them—cops can be pretty dumb—or deliberately covered them up so they wouldn't screw the DA's case. The guy was running for public office, remember, and he needed a conviction to run on. An unsolved burglary-murder would have done him no good at all.

But of the three, I like the middle one best. I've known a few Elwood Blatches in my time at Shawshank—the trigger-pullers with the crazy eyes. Such fellows want you to think they got away with the equivalent of the Hope Diamond on every caper, even if they got caught with a two-dollar Timex and nine bucks on the one they're doing time for.

And there was one thing in Tommy's story that convinced Andy beyond a shadow of a doubt. Blatch hadn't hit Quentin at random. He had called Quentin "a big rich prick," and he had *known* Quentin was a golf pro. Well, Andy and his wife had been going out to that country club for drinks and dinner once or twice a week for a couple of years, and Andy had done a considerable amount of drinking there once he found out about his wife's affair. There was a marina with the country club, and for awhile in 1947 there had been a part-time grease-and-gas jockey working there who matched Tommy's description of Elwood Blatch. A big tall man, mostly bald, with deep-set green eyes. A man who had an unpleasant way of looking at you, as though he was sizing you up. He wasn't there long, Andy said. Either he quit or Briggs, the fellow in charge of the marina, fired him. But he wasn't a man you forgot. He was too striking for that.

So Andy went to see Warden Norton on a rainy, windy day with big gray clouds scudding across the sky above the gray walls, a day when the last of the snow was starting to melt away and show lifeless patches of last year's grass in the fields beyond the prison.

The warden has a good-sized office in the Administration Wing, and behind the warden's desk there's a door which connects with the assistant warden's office. The assistant warden was out that day, but a trusty was there. He was a half-lame fellow whose real name I have forgotten; all the inmates, me included, called him Chester, after Marshal Dillon's sidekick. Chester was supposed to be watering the plants and waxing the floor. My guess is that the plants went thirsty that day and the only waxing that was done happened because of Chester's dirty ear polishing the keyhole plate of that connecting door.

He heard the warden's main door open and close and then Norton saying: "Good morning, Dufresne, how can I help you?"

"Warden," Andy began, and old Chester told us that he could hardly recognize Andy's voice it was so changed. "Warden . . . there's something . . . something's happened to me that's . . . that's so . . . so . . . I hardly know where to begin."

"Well, why don't you just begin at the beginning?" the warden said, probably in his sweetest let's-all-turn-to-the-Twenty-third-Psalm-and-read-in-unison voice. "That usually works the best."

And so Andy did. He began by refreshing Norton on the details of the crime he had been imprisoned for. Then he told the warden exactly what Tommy Williams had told him. He also gave out Tommy's name, which you may think wasn't so wise in light of later developments, but I'd just ask you what else he could have done, if his story was to have any credibility at all.

When he had finished, Norton was completely silent for some time. I can just see him, probably tipped back in his office chair under the picture of Governor Reed hanging on the wall, his fingers steepled, his liver lips pursed, his brow wrinkled into ladder rungs halfway to the crown of his head, his thirty-year pin gleaming mellowly.

"Yes," he said finally. "That's the damnedest story I ever heard. But I'll tell you what surprises me most about it, Dufresne."

"What's that, sir?"

"That you were taken in by it."

"Sir? I don't understand what you mean." And Chester said that Andy Dufresne, who had faced down Byron Hadley on the plate-shop roof thirteen years before, was almost floundering for words.

"Wellnow," Norton said. "It's pretty obvious to me that this young fellow Williams is impressed with you. Quite taken with you, as a matter of fact. He hears your tale of woe, and it's quite natural of him to want to . . . cheer you up, let's say. Quite natural. He's a young man, not terribly bright. Not surprising he didn't realize what a state it would put you into. Now what I suggest is—"

"Don't you think I thought of that?" Andy asked. "But I'd never told Tommy about the man working down at the marina. I never told *anyone* that—it never even crossed my mind! But Tommy's description of his cellmate and that man . . . they're *identical*!"

"Wellnow, you may be indulging in a little selective perception there," Norton said with a chuckle. Phrases like that, selective perception, are required learning for people in the penology and corrections business, and they use them all they can.

"That's not it all. Sir."

"That's your slant on it," Norton said, "but mine differs. And let's remember that I have only your word that there *was* such a man working at the Falmouth Hills Country Club back then."

"No, sir," Andy broke in again. "No, that isn't true. Because—"

"Anyway," Norton overrode him, expansive and loud, "let's

just look at it from the other end of the telescope, shall we? Suppose—just suppose, now—that there really *was* a fellow named Elwood Blotch."

"Blatch," Andy said tightly.

"Blatch, by all means. And let's say he *was* Thomas Williams's cellmate in Rhode Island. The chances are excellent that he has been released by now. *Excellent.* Why, we don't even know how much time he might have done there before he ended up with Williams, do we? Only that he was doing a six-to-twelve."

"No. We don't know how much time he'd done. But Tommy said he was a bad actor, a cut-up. I think there's a fair chance that he may still be in. Even if he's been released, the prison will have a record of his last known address, the names of his relatives—"

"And both would almost certainly be dead ends."

Andy was silent for a moment, and then he burst out: "Well, it's a *chance,* isn't it?"

"Yes, of course it is. So just for a moment, Dufresne, let's assume that Blatch exists and that he is still ensconced in the Rhode Island State Penitentiary. Now what is he going to say if we bring this kettle of fish to him in a bucket? Is he going to fall down on his knees, roll his eyes, and say: 'I did it! I did it! By all means add a life term onto my charge!'?"

"How can you be so obtuse?" Andy said, so low that Chester could barely hear. But he heard the warden just fine.

"What? What did you call me?"

"*Obtuse!*" Andy cried. "Is it deliberate?"

"Dufresne, you've taken five minutes of my time—no, seven—and I have a very busy schedule today. So I believe we'll just declare this little meeting closed and—"

"The country club will have all the old time-cards, don't you realize that?" Andy shouted. "They'll have tax-forms and W-twos and unemployment compensation forms, all with his name on them! There will be employees there now that were there then, maybe Briggs himself! It's been fifteen years, not forever! They'll remember him! *They will remember Blatch!* If I've got Tommy to testify to what Blatch told him, and Briggs to testify that Blatch was there, actually *working* at the country club, I can get a new trial! I can—"

"Guard! *Guard!* Take this man away!"

"What's the *matter* with you?" Andy said, and Chester told me he was very nearly screaming by then. "It's my life, my chance to get out, don't you see that? And you won't make a single long-distance call to at least verify Tommy's story? Listen, I'll pay for the call! I'll pay for—"

Then there was a sound of thrashing as the guards grabbed him and started to drag him out.

"Solitary," Warden Norton said dryly. He was probably fingering his thirty-year pin as he said it. "Bread and water."

And so they dragged Andy away, totally out of control now, still screaming at the warden; Chester said you could hear him even after the door was shut: *"It's my life! It's my life, don't you understand it's my life?"*

Twenty days on the grain and drain train for Andy down there in solitary. It was his second jolt in solitary, and his dust-up with Norton was his first real black mark since he had joined our happy family.

I'll tell you a little bit about Shawshank's solitary while we're on the subject. It's something of a throwback to those hardy pioneer days of the early to mid-1700s in Maine. In those days no one wasted much time with such things as "penology" and "rehabilitation" and "selective perception." In those days, you were taken care of in terms of absolute black and white. You were either guilty or innocent. If you were guilty, you were either hung or put in gaol. And if you were sentenced to gaol, you did not go to an institution. No, you dug your own gaol with a spade provided by the Province of Maine. You dug it as wide and as deep as you could during the period between sunup and sundown. Then they gave you a couple of skins and a bucket, and down you went. Once down, the gaoler would bar the top of your hole, throw down some grain or maybe a piece of maggoty meat once or twice a week, and maybe there would be a dipperful of barley soup on Sunday night. You pissed in the bucket, and you held up the same bucket for water when the gaoler came around at six in the morning. When it rained, you used the bucket to bail out your gaol-cell . . . unless, that is, you wanted to drown like a rat in a rainbarrel.

No one spent a long time "in the hole" as it was called; thirty months was an unusually long term, and so far as I've been able to tell, the longest term ever spent from which an inmate actually emerged alive was served by the so-called "Durham Boy," a fourteen-year-old psychopath who castrated a schoolmate with a piece of rusty metal. He did seven years, but of course he went in young and strong.

You have to remember that for a crime that was more serious than petty theft or blasphemy or forgetting to put a snot-rag in your pocket when out of doors on the Sabbath, you were hung. For low crimes such as those just mentioned and for others like them, you'd do your three or six or nine months in the hole and come out fishbelly white, cringing from the wide-open spaces, your eyes half-blind, your teeth more than likely rocking and rolling in their sockets from the scurvy, your feet crawling with fungus. Jolly old Province of Maine. Yo-ho-ho and a bottle of rum.

Shawshank's Solitary Wing was nowhere as bad as that. . . I guess. Things come in three major degrees in the human experience, I think. There's good, bad, and terrible. And as you go down into progressive darkness toward terrible, it gets harder and harder to make subdivisions.

To get to Solitary Wing you were led down twenty-three steps to a basement level where the only sound was the drip of water. The only light was supplied by a series of dangling sixty-watt bulbs. The cells were keg-shaped, like those wall-safes rich people sometimes hide behind a picture. Like a safe, the round doorways were hinged, and solid instead of barred. You got ventilation from above, but no light except for your own sixty-watt bulb, which was turned off from a master-switch promptly at 8:00 p.m., an hour before lights-out in the rest of the prison. The lightbulb wasn't in a wire mesh cage or anything like that. The feeling was that if you wanted to exist down there in the dark, you were welcome to it. Not many did . . . but after eight, of course, you had no choice. You had a bunk bolted to the wall and a can with no toilet seat. You had three ways to spend your time: sitting, shitting, or sleeping. Big choice. Twenty days could get to seem like a year. Thirty days could seem like two, and forty days like ten. Sometimes you could hear rats in the ventilation system. In a situation like that, subdivisions of terrible tend to get lost.

If anything at all can be said in favor of solitary, it's just that you get time to think. Andy had twenty days in which to think while he enjoyed his grain and drain, and when he got out he requested another meeting with the warden. Request denied. Such a meeting, the warden told him, would be "counter-productive." That's another of those phrases you have to master before you can go to work in the prisons and corrections field.

Patiently, Andy renewed his request. And renewed it. And renewed it. He had changed, had Andy Dufresne. Suddenly, as that spring of 1963 bloomed around us, there were lines in his face and sprigs of gray showing in his hair. He had lost that little trace of a smile that always seemed to linger around his mouth. His eyes stared out into space more often, and you get to know that when a man stares that way, he is counting up the years served, the months, the weeks, the days.

He renewed his request and renewed it. He was patient. He had nothing but time. It got to be summer. In Washington, President Kennedy was promising a fresh assault on poverty and on civil rights inequalities, not knowing he had only half a year to live. In Liverpool, a musical group called The Beatles was emerging as a force to be reckoned with in British music, but I guess that no one Stateside had yet heard of them. The Boston Red Sox, still four years away from what New England folks call The Miracle of '67, were languishing in the cellar of the American League. All of those things were going on out in a larger world where people walked free.

Norton saw him near the end of June, and this conversation I heard about from Andy himself some seven years later.

"If it's the squeeze, you don't have to worry," Andy told Norton in a low voice. "Do you think I'd talk that up? I'd be cutting my own throat. I'd be just as indictable as—"

"That's enough," Norton interrupted. His face was as long and cold as a slate gravestone. He leaned back in his office chair until the back of his head almost touched the sampler reading HIS JUDGMENT COMETH AND THAT RIGHT EARLY.

"But—"

"Don't you ever mention money to me again," Norton said. "Not in this office, not anywhere. Not unless you want to see that library turned back into a storage room and paint-locker again. Do you understand?"

"I was trying to set your mind at ease, that's all."

"Wellnow, when I need a sorry son of a bitch like you to set my mind at ease, I'll retire. I agreed to this appointment because I got tired of being pestered, Dufresne. I want it to stop. If you want to buy this particular Brooklyn Bridge, that's your affair. Don't make it mine. I could hear crazy stories like yours twice a week if I wanted to lay myself open to them. Every sinner in this place would be using me for a crying towel. I had more respect for you. But this is the end. The end. Have we got an understanding?"

"Yes," Andy said. "But I'll be hiring a lawyer, you know."

"What in God's name for?"

"I think we can put it together," Andy said. "With Tommy Williams and with my testimony and corroborative testimony from records and employees at the country club, I think we can put it together."

"Tommy Williams is no longer an inmate of this facility."

"*What?*"

"He's been transferred."

"Transferred *where?*"

"Cashman."

At that, Andy fell silent. He was an intelligent man, but it would have taken an extraordinarily stupid man not to smell *deal* all over that. Cashman was a minimum-security prison far up north in Aroostook County. The inmates pick a lot of potatoes, and that's hard work, but they are paid a decent wage for their labor and they can attend classes at CVI, a pretty decent vocational-technical institute, if they so desire. More important to a fellow like Tommy, a fellow with a young wife and a child, Cashman had a furlough program . . . which meant a chance to live like a normal man, at least on the weekends. A chance to build a model plane with his kid, have sex with his wife, maybe go on a picnic.

Norton had almost surely dangled all of that under Tommy's nose with only one string attached: not one more word about Elwood Blatch, not now, not ever. Or you'll end up doing hard time in Thomaston down there on scenic Route 1 with the real hard guys, and instead of having sex with your wife you'll be having it with some old bull queer.

"But why?" Andy said. "Why would—"

"As a favor to you," Norton said calmly, "I checked with Rhode Island. They did have an inmate named Elwood Blatch. He was given what they call a PP—provisional parole, another one of these crazy liberal programs to put criminals out on the streets. He's since disappeared."

Andy said: "The warden down there . . . is he a friend of yours?"

Sam Norton gave Andy a smile as cold as a deacon's watch-chain. "We are acquainted," he said.

"Why?" Andy repeated. "Can't you tell me why you did it? You knew I wasn't going to talk about. . . about anything you might have had going. You *knew* that. So *why?"*

"Because people like you make me sick," Norton said deliberately. "I like you right where you are, Mr. Dufresne, and as long as I am warden here at Shawshank, you are going to be right here. You see, you used to think that you were better than anyone else. I have gotten pretty good at seeing that on a man's face. I marked it on yours the first time I walked into the library. It might as well have been written on your forehead in capital letters. That look is gone now, and I like that just fine. It is not just that you are a useful vessel, never think that. It is simply that men like you need to learn humility. Why, you used to walk around that exercise yard as if it was a living room and you were at one of those cocktail parties where the hellbound walk around coveting each others' wives and husbands and getting swinishly drunk. But you don't walk around that way anymore. And I'll be watching to see if you should start to walk that way again. Over a period of years, I'll be watching you with great pleasure. Now get the hell out of here."

"Okay. But all the extracurricular activities stop now, Norton. The investment counseling, the scams, the free tax advice. It all stops. Get H and R Block to tell you how to declare your income."

Warden Norton's face first went brick-red . . . and then all the color fell out of it. "You're going back into solitary for that. Thirty days. Bread and water. Another black mark. And while you're in, think about this: if *anything* that's been going on should stop, the library goes. I will make it my personal business to see that it goes back to what it was before you came here. And I will make your life . . . very hard. Very difficult. You'll do the hardest time it's possible to do. You'll lose that one-bunk Hilton down in Cellblock Five, for starters, and you'll lose those rocks on the windowsill, and you'll lose any protection the guards have given you against the sodomites. You will . . . lose everything. Clear?"

I guess it was clear enough.

Time continued to pass—the oldest trick in the world, and maybe the only one that really is magic. But Andy Dufresne had changed. He had grown harder. That's the only way I can think of to put it. He went on doing Warden Norton's dirty work and he held onto the library, so outwardly things were about the same. He continued to have his birthday drinks and his year-end holiday drinks; he continued to share out the rest of each bottle. I got him fresh rock-polishing cloths from time to time, and in 1967 I got him a new rock-hammer—the one I'd gotten him nineteen years ago had, as I told you, plumb worn out. *Nineteen years!* When you say it sudden like that, those three syllables sound like the thud and double-locking of a tomb door. The rock-hammer, which had been a ten-dollar item back then, went for twenty-two by '67. He and I had a sad little grin over that.

Andy continued to shape and polish the rocks he found in the exercise yard, but the yard was smaller by then; half of what had been there in 1950 had been asphalted over in 1962. Nonetheless, he found enough to keep him occupied, I guess. When he had finished with each rock he would put it carefully on his window ledge, which faced east. He told me he liked to look at them in the sun, the pieces of the planet he had taken up from the dirt and shaped. Schists, quartzes, granites. Funny little mica-sculptures that were held together with airplane glue. Various sedimentary conglomerates that were polished and cut in such a way that you could see why Andy called them "millennium sandwiches"—the layers of different material that had built up over a period of decades and centuries.

Andy would give his stones and his rock-sculptures away from time to time in order to make room for new ones. He gave me the greatest number, I think—counting the stones that looked like matched cufflinks, I had five. There was one of the mica-sculptures I told you about, carefully crafted to look like a man throwing a javelin, and two of the sedimentary conglomerates, all the levels showing in smoothly polished cross-section. I've still got them, and I take them down every so often and think about what a man can do, if he has time enough and the will to use it, a drop at a time.

So, on the outside, at least, things were about the same. If Norton had wanted to break Andy as badly as he had said, he would have had to look below the surface to see the change. But if he *had* seen how different Andy had become, I think Norton would have been well-satisfied with the four years following his clash with Andy.

He had told Andy that Andy walked around the exercise yard as if he were at a cocktail party. That isn't the way I would have put it, but I know what he meant. It goes back to what I said about Andy wearing his freedom like an invisible coat, about how he never really developed a prison mentality. His eyes never got that dull look. He never developed the walk that men get when the day is over and they are going back to their cells for another endless night—that flat-footed, hump-shouldered walk. Andy walked with his shoulders squared, and his step was always light, as if he were heading home to a good home-cooked meal and a good woman instead of to a tasteless mess of soggy vegetables, lumpy mashed potato, and a slice or two of that fatty, gristly stuff most of the cons called mystery meat . . . that, and a picture of Raquel Welch on the wall.

But for those four years, although he never became *exactly* like the others, he did become silent, introspective, and brooding. Who could blame him? So maybe it was Warden Norton who was pleased . . . at least, for awhile.

His dark mood broke around the time of the 1967 World Series. That was the dream year, the year the Red Sox won the pennant instead of placing ninth, as the Las Vegas bookies had predicted. When it happened—when they won the American League pennant—a kind of ebullience engulfed the whole prison. There was a goofy sort of feeling that if the Dead Sox could come to life, then maybe *anybody* could do it. I can't explain that feeling now, any more than an ex-Beatlemaniac could explain *that* madness, I suppose. But it was real. Every radio in the place was tuned to the games as the Red Sox pounded down the stretch. There was gloom when the Sox dropped a pair in Cleveland near the end, and a nearly riotous joy when Rico Petrocelli put away the pop fly that clinched it. And then there was the gloom that came when Lonborg was beaten in the seventh game of the Series to end the dream just short of complete fruition. It probably pleased Norton to no end, the son of a bitch. He liked his prison wearing sackcloth and ashes.

But for Andy, there was no tumble back down into gloom. He wasn't much of a baseball fan anyway, and maybe that was why. Nevertheless, he seemed to have caught the current of good feeling, and for him it didn't peter out again after the last game of the Series. He had taken that invisible coat out of the closet and put it on again.

I remember one bright-gold fall day in very late October, a couple of weeks after the World Series had ended. It must have been a Sunday, because the exercise yard was full of men "walking off the week"—tossing a Frisbee or two, passing around a football, bartering what they had to barter. Others would be at the long table in the Visitors' Hall, under the watchful eyes of the screws, talking with their relatives, smoking cigarettes, telling sincere lies, receiving their picked-over care-packages.

Andy was squatting Indian fashion against the wall, chunking two small rocks together in his hands, his face turned up into the sunlight. It was surprisingly warm, that sun, for a day so late in the year.

"Hello, Red," he called. "Come on and sit a spell."

I did.

"You want this?" he asked, and handed me one of the two carefully polished "millennium sandwiches" I just told you about.

"I sure do," I said. "It's very pretty. Thank you."

He shrugged and changed the subject. "Big anniversary coming up for you next year."

I nodded. Next year would make me a thirty-year man. Sixty per cent of my life spent in Shawshank State Prison.

"Think you'll ever get out?"

"Sure. When I have a long white beard and just about three marbles left rolling around upstairs."

He smiled a little and then turned his face up into the sun again, his eyes closed. "Feels good."

"I think it always does when you know the damn winter's almost right on top of you."

He nodded, and we were silent for awhile.

"When I get out of here," Andy said finally, "I'm going where it's warm all the time." He spoke with such calm assurance you would have thought he had only a month or so left to serve. "You know where I'm goin, Red?"

"Nope."

"Zihuatanejo," he said, rolling the word softly from his tongue like music. "Down in Mexico. It's a little place maybe twenty miles from Playa Azul and Mexico Highway Thirty-seven. It's a hundred miles northwest of Acapulco on the Pacific Ocean. You know what the Mexicans say about the Pacific?"

I told him I didn't.

"They say it has no memory. And that's where I want to finish out my life, Red. In a warm place that has no memory."

He had picked up a handful of pebbles as he spoke; now he tossed them, one by one, and watched them bounce and roll across the baseball diamond's dirt infield, which would be under a foot of snow before long.

"Zihuatanejo. I'm going to have a little hotel down there. Six cabanas along the beach, and six more set further back, for the highway trade. I'll have a guy who'll take my guests out charter-fishing. There'll be a trophy for the guy who catches the biggest marlin of the season, and I'll put his picture up in the lobby. It won't be a family place. It'll be a place for people on their honeymoons . . . first or second varieties."

"And where are you going to get the money to buy this fabulous place?" I asked. "Your stock account?"

He looked at me and smiled. "That's not so far wrong," he said. "Sometimes you startle me, Red."

"What are you talking about?"

"There are really only two types of men in the world when it comes to bad trouble," Andy said, cupping a match between his hands and lighting a cigarette. "Suppose there was a house full of rare paintings and sculptures and fine old antiques, Red? And suppose the guy who owned the house heard that there was a monster of a hurricane headed right at it? One of those two kinds of men just hopes for the best. The hurricane will change course, he says to himself. No right-thinking hurricane would ever dare wipe out all these Rembrandts, my two Degas horses, my Grant Woods, and my Bentons. Furthermore, God wouldn't allow it. And if worse comes to worst, they're insured. That's one sort of man. The other sort just assumes that hurricane is going to tear right through the middle of his house. If the weather bureau says the hurricane just changed course, this guy assumes it'll change back in order to put his house on ground-zero again. This second type of guy knows there's no harm in hoping for the best as long as you're prepared for the worst."

I lit a cigarette of my own. "Are you saying you prepared for the eventuality?"

"Yes. I prepared for the *hurricane.* I knew how bad it looked. I didn't have much time, but in the time I had, I operated. I had a friend—just about the only person who stood by me—who worked for an investment company in Portland. He died about six years ago."

"Sorry."

"Yeah." Andy tossed his butt away. "Linda and I had about fourteen thousand dollars. Not a big bundle, but hell, we were young. We had our whole lives ahead of us." He grimaced a little, then laughed. "When the shit hit the fan, I started lugging my Rembrandts out of the path of the hurricane. I sold my stocks and paid the capital gains tax just like a good little boy. Declared everything. Didn't cut any corners."

"Didn't they freeze your estate?"

"I was charged with murder, Red, not dead! You can't freeze the assets of an innocent man—thank God. And it was awhile before they even got brave enough to charge me with the crime. Jim—my friend—and I, we had some time. I got hit pretty good, just dumping everything like that. Got my nose skinned. But at the time I had worse things to worry about than a small skinning on the stock market."

"Yeah, I'd say you did."

"But when I came to Shawshank it was all safe. It's still safe. Outside these walls, Red, there's a man that no living soul has ever seen face to face. He has a Social Security card and a Maine driver's license. He's got a birth certificate. Name of Peter Stevens. Nice, anonymous name, huh?"

"Who is he?" I asked. I thought I knew what he was going to say, but I couldn't believe it.

"Me."

"You're not going to tell me that you had time to set up a false identity while the bulls were sweating you," I said, "or that you finished the job while you were on trial for—"

"No, I'm not going to tell you that. My friend Jim was the one who set up the false identity. He started after my appeal was turned down, and the major pieces of identification were in his hands by the spring of 1950."

"He must have been a pretty close friend," I said. I was not sure how much of this I believed—a little, a lot, or none. But the day was warm and the sun was out, and it was one hell of a good story. "All of that's one hundred per cent illegal, setting up a false ID like that."

"He was a close friend," Andy said. "We were in the war together. France, Germany, the occupation. He was a good friend. He knew it was illegal, but he also knew that setting up a false identity in this country is very easy and very safe. He took my money—my money with all the taxes on it paid so the IRS wouldn't get too interested—and invested it for Peter Stevens. He did that in 1950 and 1951. Today it amounts to three hundred and seventy thousand dollars, plus change."

I guess my jaw made a thump when it dropped against my chest, because he smiled.

"Think of all the things people wish they'd invested in since 1950 or so, and two or three of them will be things Peter Stevens was into. If I hadn't ended up in here, I'd probably be worth seven or eight million bucks by now. I'd have a Rolls . . . and probably an ulcer as big as a portable radio."

His hands went to the dirt and began sifting out more pebbles. They moved gracefully, restlessly.

"It was hoping for the best and expecting the worst—nothing but that. The false name was just to keep what little capital I had untainted. It was lugging the paintings out of the path of the hurricane. But I had no idea that the hurricane . . . that it could go on as long as it has."

I didn't say anything for awhile. I guess I was trying to absorb the idea that this small, spare man in prison gray next to me could be worth more money than Warden Norton would make in the rest of his miserable life, even with the scams thrown in.

"When you said you could get a lawyer, you sure weren't kidding," I said at last. "For that kind of dough you could have hired Clarence Darrow, or whoever's passing for him these days. Why didn't you, Andy? Christ! You could have been out of here like a rocket."

He smiled. It was the same smile that had been on his face

when he'd told me he and his wife had had their whole lives ahead of them. "No," he said.

"A good lawyer would have sprung the Williams kid from Cashman whether he wanted to go or not," I said. I was getting carried away now. "You could have gotten your new trial, hired private detectives to look for that guy Blatch, and blown Norton out of the water to boot. Why not, Andy?"

"Because I outsmarted myself. If I ever try to put my hands on Peter Stevens's money from inside here, I'll lose every cent of it. My friend Jim could have arranged it, but Jim's dead. You see the problem?"

I saw it. For all the good that money could do Andy, it might as well have really belonged to another person. In a way, it did. And if the stuff it was invested in suddenly turned bad, all Andy could do would be to watch the plunge, to trace it day after day on the stocks-and-bonds page of the *Press-Herald*. It's a tough life if you don't weaken, I guess.

"I'll tell you how it is, Red. There's a big hayfield in the town of Buxton. You know where Buxton is at, don't you?"

I said I did. It lies right next door to Scarborough.

"That's right. And at the north end of this particular hayfield there's a rock wall, right out of a Robert Frost poem. And somewhere along the base of that wall is a rock that has no business in a Maine hayfield. It's a piece of volcanic glass, and until 1947 it was a paperweight on my office desk. My friend Jim put it in that wall. There's a key underneath it. The key opens a safe deposit box in the Portland branch of the Casco Bank."

"I guess you're in a peck of trouble," I said. "When your friend Jim died, the IRS must have opened all of his safe deposit boxes. Along with the executor of his will, of course."

Andy smiled and tapped the side of my head. "Not bad. There's more up there than marshmallows, I guess. But we took care of the possibility that Jim might die while I was in the slam. The box is in the Peter Stevens name, and once a year the firm of lawyers that served as Jim's executors sends a check to the Casco to cover the rental of the Stevens box.

"Peter Stevens is inside that box, just waiting to get out. His birth certificate, his Social Security card, and his driver's license. The license is six years out of date because Jim died six years ago, true, but it's still perfectly renewable for a five-dollar fee. His stock certificates are there, the tax-free municipals, and about eighteen bearer bonds in the amount of ten thousand dollars each."

I whistled.

"Peter Stevens is locked in a safe deposit box at the Casco Bank in Portland and Andy Dufresne is locked in a safe deposit box at Shawshank," he said. "Tit for tat. And the key that unlocks the box and the money and the new life is under a hunk of black glass in a Buxton hayfield. Told you this much, so I'll tell you something else, Red—for the last twenty years, give or take, I have been watching the papers with a more than usual interest for news of any construction project in Buxton. I keep thinking that someday soon I'm going to read that they're putting a highway through there, or erecting a new community hospital, or building a shopping center. Burying my new life under ten feet of concrete, or spitting it into a swamp somewhere with a big load of fill."

I blurted, "Jesus Christ, Andy, if all of this is true, how do you keep from going crazy?"

He smiled. "So far, all quiet on the Western front."

"But it could be years—"

"It will be. But maybe not as many as the State and Warden Norton think it's going to be. I just can't afford to wait that long. I keep thinking about Zihuatanejo and that small hotel. That's all I want from my life now, Red, and I don't think that's too much to want. I didn't kill Glenn Quentin and I didn't kill my wife, and that hotel . . . it's not too much to want. To swim and get a tan and sleep in a room with open windows and *space* . . . that's not too much to want."

He slung the stones away.

"You know, Red," he said in an offhand voice. "A place like that . . . I'd have to have a man who knows how to get things."

I thought about it for a long time. And the biggest drawback in my mind wasn't even that we were talking pipedreams in a shitty little prison exercise yard with armed guards looking down at us from their sentry posts. "I couldn't do it," I said. "I couldn't get along on the outside. I'm what they call an institutional man now. In here I'm the man who can get it for you, yeah. But out there, anyone can get it for you. Out there, if you want posters or rock-hammers or one particular record or a boat-in-a-bottle model kit, you can use the fucking Yellow Pages. In here, *I'm* the fucking Yellow Pages. I wouldn't know how to begin. Or where."

"You underestimate yourself," he said. "You're a self-educated man, a self-made man. A rather remarkable man, I think."

"Hell, I don't even have a high school diploma."

"I know that," he said. "But it isn't just a piece of paper that makes a man. And it isn't just prison that breaks one, either."

"I couldn't hack it outside, Andy. I know that."

He got up. "You think it over," he said casually, just as the inside whistle blew. And he strolled off, as if he were a free man who had just made another free man a proposition. And for awhile just that was enough to make me *feel* free. Andy could do that. He could make me forget for a time that we were both lifers, at the mercy of a hard-ass parole board and a psalm-singing warden who liked Andy Dufresne right where he was. After all, Andy was a lap-dog who could do tax-returns. What a wonderful animal!

But by that night in my cell I felt like a prisoner again. The whole idea seemed absurd, and that mental image of blue water and white beaches seemed more cruel than foolish—it dragged at my brain like a fishhook. I just couldn't wear that invisible coat the way Andy did. I fell asleep that night and dreamed of a great glassy black stone in the middle of a hayfield; a stone shaped like a giant blacksmith's anvil. I was trying to rock the stone up so I could get the key that was underneath. It wouldn't budge; it was just too damned big.

And in the background, but getting closer, I could hear the baying of bloodhounds.

Which leads us, I guess, to the subject of jailbreaks.

Sure, they happen from time to time in our happy little family. You don't go over the wall, though, not at Shawshank, not if you're smart. The searchlight beams go all night, probing long white fingers across the open fields that surround the prison on three sides and the stinking marshland on the fourth. Cons do go over the wall from time to time, and the searchlights almost always catch them. If not, they get picked up trying to thumb a ride on Highway 6 or Highway 99. If they try to cut across country, some farmer sees them and just phones the location in to the prison. Cons who go over the wall are stupid cons. Shawshank is no Canon City, but in a rural area a man humping his ass across country in a gray pajama suit sticks out like a cockroach on a wedding cake.

Over the years, the guys who have done the best—maybe oddly, maybe not so oddly—are the guys who did it on the spur of the moment. Some of them have gone out in the middle of a cartful of sheets; a convict sandwich on white, you could say. There was a lot of that when I first came in here, but over the years they have more or less closed that loophole.

Warden Norton's famous "Inside-Out" program produced its share of escapees, too. They were the guys who decided they liked what lay to the right of the hyphen better than what lay to the left. And again, in most cases it was a very casual kind of thing. Drop your blueberry rake and stroll into the bushes while one of the screws is having a glass of water at the truck or when a couple of them get too involved in arguing over yards passing or rushing on the old Boston Patriots.

In 1969, the Inside-Outers were picking potatoes in Sabbatus. It was the third of November and the work was almost done. There was a guard named Henry Pugh—and he is no longer a member of our happy little family, believe me—sitting on the back bumper of one of the potato trucks and having his lunch with his carbine across his knees when a beautiful (or so it was told to me, but sometimes these things get exaggerated) ten-point buck strolled out of the cold early afternoon mist. Pugh went after it with visions of just how that trophy would look mounted in his rec room, and while he was doing it, three of his charges just walked away. Two were recaptured in a Lisbon Falls pinball parlor. The third has not been found to this day.

I suppose the most famous case of all was that of Sid Nedeau. This goes back to 1958, and I guess it will never be topped. Sid was out lining the ballfield for a Saturday intramural baseball game when the three o'clock inside whistle blew, signalling the shift-change for the guards. The parking lot is just beyond the exercise yard, on the other side of the electrically operated main gate. At three the gate opens and the guards coming on duty and those going off mingle. There's a lot of back-slapping and bullyragging, comparison of league bowling scores and the usual number of tired old ethnic jokes.

Sid just trundled his lining machine right out through the gate, leaving a three-inch baseline all the way from home plate in the exercise yard to the ditch on the far side of Route 6, where they found the machine overturned in a pile of lime. Don't ask me how he did it. He was dressed in his prison uniform, he stood six-feet-two, and he was billowing clouds of lime-dust behind him. All I can figure is that, it being Friday afternoon and all, the guards going off were so happy to be going off, and the guards coming on were so downhearted to be coming on, that the members of the former group never got their heads out of the clouds and those in the latter never got their noses off their shoetops . . . and old Sid Nedeau just sort of slipped out between the two.

So far as I know, Sid is still at large. Over the years, Andy Dufresne and I had a good many laughs over Sid Nedeau's great escape, and when we heard about that airline hijacking for ransom, the one where the guy parachuted from the back door of the airplane, Andy swore up and down that D. B. Cooper's real name was Sid Nedeau.

"And he probably had a pocketful of baseline lime in his pocket for good luck," Andy said. "That lucky son of a bitch."

But you should understand that a case like Sid Nedeau, or the fellow who got away clean from the Sabbatus potato-field crew, guys like that are winning the prison version of the Irish Sweepstakes. Purely a case of six different kinds of luck somehow jelling together all at the same moment. A stiff like Andy could wait ninety years and not get a similar break.

Maybe you remember, a ways back, I mentioned a guy named Henley Backus, the washroom foreman in the laundry. He came to Shawshank in 1922 and died in the prison infirmary thirty-one years later. Escapes and escape attempts were a hobby of his, maybe because he never quite dared to take the plunge himself. He could tell you a hundred different schemes, all of them crackpot, and all of them had been tried in The Shank at one time or another. My favorite was the tale of Beaver Morrison, a b&e convict who tried to build a glider from scratch in the plate-factory basement. The plans he was working from were in a circa-1900 book called *The Modern Boy's Guide to Fun and Adventure*. Beaver got it built without being discovered, or so the story goes, only to discover there was no door from the basement big enough to get the damned thing out. When Henley told that story, you could bust a gut laughing, and he knew a dozen—no, two dozen—almost as funny.

When it came to detailing Shawshank bust-outs, Henley had it down chapter and verse. He told me once that during his time there had been better than four hundred escape attempts *that he knew of.* Really think about that for a moment before you just nod your head and read on. Four *hundred* escape attempts! That comes out to 12.9 escape attempts for every year Henley Backus was in Shawshank and keeping track of them. The Escape-Attempt-of-the-Month Club. Of course most of them were pretty slipshod affairs, the sort of thing that ends up with a guard grabbing some poor, sidling slob's arm and growling, "Where do you think *you're* going, you happy asshole?"

Henley said he'd class maybe sixty of them as more serious attempts, and he included the "prison break" of 1937, the year before I arrived at The Shank. The new Administration Wing was under construction then and fourteen cons got out, using construction equipment in a poorly locked shed. The whole of southern Maine got into a panic over those fourteen "hardened criminals," most of whom were scared to death and had no more idea of where they should go than a jackrabbit does when it's headlight-pinned to the highway with a big truck bearing down on it. Not one of those fourteen got away. Two of them were shot dead—by civilians, not police officers or prison personnel—but none got away.

How many *had* gotten away between 1938, when I came here, and that day in October when Andy first mentioned Zihuatanejo to me? Putting my information and Henley's together, I'd say ten. Ten that got away clean. And although it isn't the kind of thing you can know for sure, I'd guess that at least half of those ten are doing time in other institutions of lower learning like The Shank. Because you *do* get institutionalized. When you take away a man's freedom and teach him to live in a cell, he seems to lose his ability to think in dimensions. He's like that jackrabbit I mentioned, frozen in the oncoming lights of the truck that is bound to kill it. More often than not a con who's just out will pull some dumb job that hasn't a chance in hell of succeeding . . . and why? Because it'll get him back inside. Back where he understands how things work.

Andy wasn't that way, but I was. The idea of seeing the

Pacific *sounded* good, but I was afraid that actually being there would scare me to death—the bigness of it.

Anyhow, the day of that conversation about Mexico, and about Mr. Peter Stevens . . . that was the day I began to believe that Andy had some idea of doing a disappearing act. I hoped to God he would be careful if he did, and still, I wouldn't have bet money on his chances of succeeding. Warden Norton, you see, was watching Andy with a special close eye. Andy wasn't just another deadhead with a number to Norton; they had a working relationship, you might say. Also, Andy had brains and he had heart. Norton was determined to use the one and crush the other.

As there are honest politicians on the outside—ones who stay bought—there are honest prison guards, and if you are a good judge of character and if you have some loot to spread around, I suppose it's possible that you could buy enough look-the-other-way to make a break. I'm not the man to tell you such a thing has never been done, but Andy Dufresne wasn't the man who could do it. Because, as I've said, Norton was watching. Andy knew it, and the screws knew it, too.

Nobody was going to nominate Andy for the Inside-Out program, not as long as Warden Norton was evaluating the nominations. And Andy was not the kind of man to try a casual Sid Nedeau type of escape.

If I had been him, the thought of that key would have tormented me endlessly. I would have been lucky to get two hours' worth of honest shut-eye a night. Buxton was less than thirty miles from Shawshank. So near and yet so far.

I still thought his best chance was to engage a lawyer and try for the retrial. Anything to get out from under Norton's thumb. Maybe Tommy Williams could be shut up by nothing more than a cushy furlough program, but I wasn't entirely sure. Maybe a good old Mississippi hard-ass lawyer could crack him . . . and maybe that lawyer wouldn't even have to work that hard. Williams had honestly liked Andy. Every now and then I'd bring these points up to Andy, who would only smile, his eyes far away, and say he was thinking about it.

Apparently he'd been thinking about a lot of other things, as well.

In 1975, Andy Dufresne escaped from Shawshank. He hasn't been recaptured, and I don't think he ever will be. In fact, I don't think Andy Dufresne even exists anymore. But I think there's a man down in Zihuatanejo, Mexico, named Peter Stevens. Probably running a very new small hotel in this year of our Lord 1976.

I'll tell you what I know and what I think; that's about all I can do, isn't it?

On March 12th, 1975, the cell doors in Cellblock 5 opened at 6:30 a.m., as they do every morning around here except Sunday. And as they do every day except Sunday, the inmates of those cells stepped forward into the corridor and formed two lines as the cell doors slammed shut behind them. They walked up to the main cellblock gate, where they were counted off by two guards before being sent on down to the cafeteria for a breakfast of oatmeal, scrambled eggs, and fatty bacon.

All of this went according to routine until the count at the cellblock gate. There should have been twenty-seven. Instead, there were twenty-six. After a call to the Captain of the Guards, Cellblock 5 was allowed to go to breakfast.

The Captain of the Guards, a not half-bad fellow named Richard Gonyar, and his assistant, a jolly prick named Dave Burkes, came down to Cellblock 5 right away. Gonyar reopened the cell doors and he and Burkes went down the corridor together, dragging their sticks over the bars, their guns out. In a case like that what you usually have is someone who has been taken sick in the night, so sick he can't even step out of his cell in the morning. More rarely, someone has died . . . or committed suicide.

But this time, they found a mystery instead of a sick man

or a dead man. They found no man at all. There were fourteen cells in Cellblock 5, seven to a side, all fairly neat—restriction of visiting privileges is the penalty for a sloppy cell at Shawshank—and all very empty.

Gonyar's first assumption was that there had been a miscount or a practical joke. So instead of going off to work after breakfast, the inmates of Cellblock 5 were sent back to their cells, joking and happy. Any break in the routine was always welcome.

Cell doors opened; prisoners stepped in; cell doors closed. Some clown shouting, "I want my lawyer, I want my lawyer, you guys run this place just like a frigging prison."

Burkes: "Shut up in there, or I'll rank you."

The clown: "I ranked your wife, Burkie."

Gonyar: "Shut up, all of you, or you'll spend the day in there."

He and Burkes went up the line again, counting noses. They didn't have to go far.

"Who belongs in this cell?" Gonyar asked the rightside night guard.

"Andrew Dufresne," the rightside answered, and that was all it took. Everything stopped being routine right then. The balloon went up.

In all the prison movies I've seen, this wailing horn goes off when there's been a break. That never happens at Shawshank. The first thing Gonyar did was to get in touch with the warden. The second thing was to get a search of the prison going. The third was to alert the state police in Scarborough to the possibility of a breakout.

That was the routine. It didn't call for them to search the suspected escapee's cell, and so no one did. Not then. Why would they? It was a case of what you see is what you get. It was a small square room, bars on the window and bars on the sliding door. There was a toilet and an empty cot. Some pretty rocks on the windowsill.

And the poster, of course. It was Linda Ronstadt by then.

The poster was right over his bunk. There had been a poster there, in that exact same place, for twenty-six years. And when someone—it was Warden Norton himself, as it turned out, poetic justice if there ever was any—looked behind it, they got one hell of a shock.

But that didn't happen until six-thirty that night, almost twelve hours after Andy had been reported missing, probably twenty hours after he had actually made his escape.

Norton hit the roof.

I have it on good authority—Chester, the trusty, who was waxing the hall floor in the Admin Wing that day. He didn't have to polish any keyplates with his ear that day; he said you could hear the warden clear down to Records & Files as he chewed on Rich Gonyar's ass.

"What do you mean, you're 'satisfied he's not on the prison grounds'? What does that mean? It means you didn't find him! You better find him! You better! Because I want him! Do you hear me? I want him!"

Gonyar said something.

"Didn't happen on your shift? That's what *you* say. So far as *I* can tell, no one knows *when* it happened. Or how. Or if it really did. Now, I want him in my office by three o'clock this afternoon, or some heads are going to roll. I can promise you that, and I *always* keep my promises."

Something else from Gonyar, something that seemed to provoke Norton to even greater rage.

"No? Then look at this! *Look at this!* You recognize it? Last night's tally for Cellblock Five. Every prisoner accounted for! Dufresne was locked up last night at nine and it is impossible for him to be gone now! *It is impossible! Now you find him!*"

But at three that afternoon Andy was still among the missing. Norton himself stormed down to Cellblock 5 a few hours later, where the rest of us had been locked up all of that day. Had we been questioned? We had spent most of that long day being questioned by harried screws who were feeling the breath of the dragon on the backs of their necks. We all said the same thing: we had seen nothing, heard nothing. And so far as I know, we were all telling the truth. I know that I was. All we could say was that Andy had indeed been in his cell at the time of the lock-in, and at lights-out an hour later.

One wit suggested that Andy had poured himself out through the keyhole. The suggestion earned the guy four days in solitary. They were uptight.

So Norton came down—stalked down—glaring at us with blue eyes nearly hot enough to strike sparks from the tempered steel bars of our cages. He looked at us as if he believed we were all in on it. Probably he did believe it.

He went into Andy's cell and looked around. It was just as Andy had left it, the sheets on his bunk turned back but without looking slept-in. Rocks on the windowsill . . . but not all of them. The ones he liked best he took with him.

"Rocks," Norton hissed, and swept them off the window ledge with a clatter. Gonyar, who was now on overtime, winced but said nothing.

Norton's eyes fell on the Linda Ronstadt poster. Linda was looking back over her shoulder, her hands tucked into the back pockets of a very tight pair of fawn-colored slacks. She was wearing a halter and she had a deep California tan. It must have offended the hell out of Norton's Baptist sensibilities, that poster. Watching him glare at it, I remembered what Andy had once said about feeling he could almost step through the picture and be with the girl.

In a very real way, that was exactly what he did—as Norton was only seconds from discovering.

"Wretched thing!" he grunted, and ripped the poster from the wall with a single swipe of his hand.

And revealed the gaping, crumbled hole in the concrete behind it.

• • •

Gonyar wouldn't go in.

Norton ordered him—God, they must have heard Norton ordering Rich Gonyar to go in there all over the prison—and Gonyar just refused him, point blank.

"I'll have your job for this!" Norton screamed. He was as hysterical as a woman having a hot-flash. He had utterly blown his cool. His neck had turned a rich, dark red, and two veins stood out, throbbing, on his forehead. "You can count on it, you . . . you Frenchman! I'll have your job and I'll see to it that you never get another one in any prison system in New England!"

Gonyar silently held out his service pistol to Norton, butt first. He'd had enough. He was then two hours overtime, going on three, and he'd just had enough. It was as if Andy's defection from our happy little family had driven Norton right over the edge of some private irrationality that had been there for a long time . . . certainly he was crazy that night.

I don't know what that private irrationality might have been, of course. But I do know that there were twenty-six cons listening to Norton's little dust-up with Rich Gonyar that evening as the last of the light faded from a dull late-winter sky, all of us hard-timers and long-line riders who had seen the administrators come and go, the hard-asses and the candy-asses alike, and we all knew that Warden Samuel Norton had just passed what the engineers like to call "the breaking strain."

And by God, it almost seemed to me that somewhere I could hear Andy Dufresne laughing.

Norton finally got a skinny drink of water on the night shift to go into the hole that had been behind Andy's poster of Linda Ronstadt. The skinny guard's name was Rory Tremont, and he was not exactly a ball of fire in the brains department. Maybe he thought he was going to win a Bronze Star or something. As it turned out, it was fortunate that Norton got someone of

Andy's approximate height and build to go in there; if they had sent a big-assed fellow—as most prison guards seem to be—the guy would have stuck in there as sure as God made green grass . . . and he might be there still.

Tremont went in with a nylon filament rope, which someone had found in the trunk of his car, tied around his waist and a big six-battery flashlight in one hand. By then Gonyar, who had changed his mind about quitting and who seemed to be the only one there still able to think clearly, had dug out a set of blueprints. I knew well enough what they showed him—a wall which looked, in cross-section, like a sandwich. The entire wall was ten feet thick. The inner and outer sections were each about four feet thick. In the center was two feet of pipe-space, and you want to believe that was the meat of the thing . . . in more ways than one.

Tremont's voice came out of the hole, sounding hollow and dead. "Something smells awful in here, Warden."

"Never mind that! Keep going."

Tremont's lower legs disappeared into the hole. A moment later his feet were gone, too. His light flashed dimly back and forth.

"Warden, it smells pretty damn bad."

"Never *mind,* I said!" Norton cried.

Dolorously, Tremont's voice floated back: "Smells like shit. Oh God, that's what it is, it's *shit,* oh my God lemme outta here I'm gonna blow my groceries oh shit it's shit oh my *Gaw-wwwwd—*" And then came the unmistakable sound of Rory Tremont losing his last couple of meals.

Well, that was it for me. I couldn't help myself. The whole day—hell no, the last thirty *years*—all came up on me at once and I started laughing fit to split, a laugh such as I'd never had since I was a free man, the kind of laugh I never expected to have inside these gray walls. And oh dear *God* didn't it feel good!

"Get that man out of here!" Warden Norton was screaming, and I was laughing so hard I didn't know if he meant me or Tremont. I just went on laughing and kicking my feet and holding onto my belly. I couldn't have stopped if Norton had threatened to shoot me dead-bang on the spot. *"Get him OUT!"*

Well, friends and neighbors, I was the one who went. Straight down to solitary, and there I stayed for fifteen days. A long shot. But every now and then I'd think about poor old not-too-bright Rory Tremont bellowing *oh shit it's shit,* and then I'd think about Andy Dufresne heading south in his own car, dressed in a nice suit, and I'd just have to laugh. I did that fifteen days in solitary practically standing on my head. Maybe because half of me was with Andy Dufresne, Andy Dufresne who had waded in shit and came out clean on the other side, Andy Dufresne, headed for the Pacific.

I heard the rest of what went on that night from half a dozen sources. There wasn't all that much, anyway. I guess that Rory Tremont decided he didn't have much left to lose after he'd lost his lunch and dinner, because he did go on. There was no danger of falling down the pipe-shaft between the inner and outer segments of the cellblock wall; it was so narrow that Tremont actually had to wedge himself down. He said later that he could only take half-breaths and that he knew what it would be like to be buried alive.

What he found at the bottom of the shaft was a master sewer-pipe which served the fourteen toilets in Cellblock 5, a porcelain pipe that had been laid thirty-three years before. It had been broken into. Beside the jagged hole in the pipe, Tremont found Andy's rock-hammer.

Andy had gotten free, but it hadn't been easy.

The pipe was even narrower than the shaft Tremont had just descended. Rory Tremont didn't go in, and so far as I know, no one else did, either. It must have been damn near unspeakable. A rat jumped out of the pipe as Tremont was examining the hole and the rock-hammer, and he swore later that it was nearly as big as a cocker spaniel pup. He went back up the crawlspace to Andy's cell like a monkey on a stick.

Andy had gone into that pipe. Maybe he knew that it emptied into a stream five hundred yards beyond the prison on the marshy western side. I think he did. The prison blueprints were around, and Andy would have found a way to look at them. He was a methodical cuss. He would have known or found out that the sewer-pipe running out of Cellblock 5 was the last one in Shawshank not hooked into the new waste-treatment plant, and he would have known it was do it by mid-1975 or do it never, because in August they were going to switch us over to the new waste-treatment plant, too.

Five hundred yards. The length of five football fields. Just shy of half a mile. He crawled that distance, maybe with one of those small Penlites in his hand, maybe with nothing but a couple of books of matches. He crawled through foulness that I either can't imagine or don't want to imagine. Maybe the rats scattered in front of him, or maybe they went for him the way such animals sometimes will when they've had a chance to grow bold in the dark. He must have had just enough clearance at the shoulders to keep moving, and he probably had to shove himself through the places where the lengths of pipe were joined. If it had been me, the claustrophobia would have driven me mad a dozen times over. But he did it.

At the far end of the pipe they found a set of muddy footprints leading out of the sluggish, polluted creek the pipe fed into. Two miles from there a search party found his prison uniform—that was a day later.

The story broke big in the papers, as you might guess, but no one within a fifteen-mile radius of the prison stepped forward to report a stolen car, stolen clothes, or a naked man in the moonlight. There was not so much as a barking dog in a farmyard. He came out of the sewer-pipe and he disappeared like smoke.

But I am betting he disappeared in the direction of Buxton.

• • •

Three months after that memorable day, Warden Norton resigned. He was a broken man, it gives me great pleasure to report. The spring was gone from his step. On his last day he shuffled out with his head down like an old con shuffling down to the infirmary for his codeine pills. It was Gonyar who took over, and to Norton that must have seemed like the unkindest cut of all. For all I know, Sam Norton is down there in Eliot now, attending services at the Baptist church every Sunday, and wondering how the hell Andy Dufresne ever could have gotten the better of him.

I could have told him; the answer to the question is simplicity itself. Some have got it, Sam. And some don't, and never will.

That's what I know; now I'm going to tell you what I think. I may have it wrong on some of the specifics, but I'd be willing to bet my watch and chain that I've got the general outline down pretty well. Because, with Andy being the sort of man that he was, there's only one or two ways that it could have been. And every now and then, when I think it out, I think of Normaden, that half-crazy Indian. "Nice fella," Normaden had said after celling with Andy for eight months. "I was glad to go, me. Bad draft in that cell. All the time cold. He don't let nobody touch his things. That's okay. Nice man, never made fun. But big draft." Poor crazy Normaden. He knew more than all the rest of us, and he knew it sooner. And it was eight long months before Andy could get him out of there and have the cell to himself again. If it hadn't been for the eight months Normaden had spent with him after Warden Norton first came in, I do believe that Andy would have been free before Nixon resigned.

I believe now that it began in 1949, way back then—not with the rock-hammer, but with the Rita Hayworth poster. I told you how nervous he seemed when he asked for that, nervous and filled with suppressed excitement. At the time I thought it was just embarrassment, that Andy was the sort of guy who'd never want someone else to know that he had feet of clay and wanted a woman . . . especially if it was a fantasy-woman. But I think now that I was wrong. I think now that Andy's excitement came from something else altogether.

What was responsible for the hole that Warden Norton eventually found behind the poster of a girl that hadn't even been born when that photo of Rita Hayworth was taken? Andy Dufresne's perseverance and hard work, yeah—I don't take any of that away from him. But there were two other elements in the equation: a lot of luck, and WPA concrete.

You don't need me to explain the luck, I guess. The WPA concrete I checked out for myself. I invested some time and a couple of stamps and wrote first to the University of Maine History Department and then to a fellow whose address they were able to give me. This fellow had been foreman of the WPA project that built the Shawshank Max Security Wing.

The wing, which contains Cellblocks 3, 4, and 5, was built in the years 1934-37. Now, most people don't think of cement and concrete as "technological developments," the way we think of cars and old furnaces and rocket-ships, but they really are. There was no modern cement until 1870 or so, and no modern concrete until after the turn of the century. Mixing concrete is as delicate a business as making bread. You can get it too watery or not watery enough. You can get the sand-mix too thick or too thin, and the same is true of the gravel-mix. And back in 1934, the science of mixing the stuff was a lot less sophisticated than it is today.

The walls of Cellblock 5 were solid enough, but they weren't exactly dry and toasty. As a matter of fact, they were and are pretty damned dank. After a long wet spell they would sweat and sometimes even drip. Cracks had a way of appearing, some an inch deep. They were routinely mortared over.

Now here comes Andy Dufresne into Cellblock 5. He's a man who graduated from the University of Maine's school of business, but he's also a man who took two or three geology courses along the way. Geology had, in fact, become his chief hobby. I imagine it appealed to his patient, meticulous nature. A ten-thousand-year ice age here. A million years of mountain-building there. Plates of bedrock grinding against each other deep under the earth's skin over the millennia. *Pressure.* Andy told me once that all of geology is the study of pressure.

And time, of course.

He had time to study those walls. Plenty of time. When the cell door slams and the lights go out, there's nothing else to look at.

First-timers usually have a hard time adjusting to the confinement of prison life. They get screw-fever. Sometimes they have to be hauled down to the infirmary and sedated a couple of times before they get on the beam. It's not unusual to hear some new member of our happy little family banging on the bars of his cell and screaming to be let out. . . and before the cries have gone on for long, the chant starts up along the cellblock: "Fresh *fish,* hey little fishie, fresh *fish,* fresh *fish,* got fresh *fish* today!"

Andy didn't flip out like that when he came to The Shank in 1948, but that's not to say that he didn't feel many of the same things. He may have come close to madness; some do, and some go sailing right over the edge. Old life blown away in the wink of an eye, indeterminate nightmare stretching out ahead, a long season in hell.

So what did he do, I ask you? He searched almost desperately for something to divert his restless mind. Oh, there are all sorts of ways to divert yourself, even in prison; it seems like the human mind is full of an infinite number of possibilities when it comes to diversion. I told you about the sculptor and his *Three Ages of Jesus.* There were coin collectors who were always losing their collections to thieves, stamp collectors, one fellow who had postcards from thirty-five different countries—and let me tell you, he would have turned out your lights if he'd caught you diddling with his postcards.

Andy got interested in rocks. And the walls of his cell.

I think that his initial intention might have been to do no more than to carve his initials into the wall where the poster of Rita Hayworth would soon be hanging. His initials, or maybe a few lines from some poem. Instead, what he found was that interestingly weak concrete. Maybe he started to carve his initials and a big chunk of the wall just fell out. I can see him, lying there on his bunk, looking at that broken chunk of concrete, turning it over in his hands. Never mind the wreck of your whole life, never mind that you got railroaded into this place by a whole trainload of bad luck. Let's forget all that and look at this piece of concrete.

Some months further along he might have decided it would be fun to see how much of that wall he could take out. But you can't just start digging into your wall and then, when the weekly inspection (or one of the surprise inspections that are always turning up interesting caches of booze, drugs, dirty pictures, and weapons) comes around, say to the guard: "This? Just excavating a little hole in my cell wall. Not to worry, my good man."

No, he couldn't have that. So he came to me and asked if I could get him a Rita Hayworth poster. Not a little one but a big one.

And, of course, he had the rock-hammer. I remember thinking when I got him that gadget back in '48 that it would take a man six hundred years to burrow through the wall with it. True enough. But Andy only had to go through *half* the wall—and even with the soft concrete, it took him two rock-hammers and twenty-seven years to do it.

Of course he lost most of one of those years to Normaden, and he could only work at night, preferably late at night, when almost everybody is asleep—including the guards who work the night shift. But I suspect the thing which slowed him down the most was getting rid of the wall as he took it out. He could muffle the sound of his work by wrapping the head of his hammer in rock-polishing cloths, but what to do with the pulverized concrete and the occasional chunks that came out whole?

I think he must have broken up the chunks into pebbles and . . .

I remember the Sunday after I had gotten him the rock-hammer. I remember watching him walk across the exercise yard, his face puffy from his latest go-round with the sisters. I saw him stoop, pick up a pebble . . . and it disappeared up his sleeve. That inside sleeve-pocket is an old prison trick. Up your sleeve or just inside the cuff of your pants. And I have another memory, very strong but unfocused, maybe something I saw more than once. This memory is of Andy Dufresne walking across the exercise yard on a hot summer day when the air was utterly still. Still, yeah . . . except for the little breeze that seemed to be blowing sand around Andy Dufresne's feet.

So maybe he had a couple of cheaters in his pants below the knees. You loaded the cheaters up with fill and then just strolled around, your hands in your pockets, and when you felt safe and unobserved, you gave the pockets a little twitch. The pockets, of course, are attached by string or strong thread to the cheaters. The fill goes cascading out of your pantslegs as you walk. The World War II POWs who were trying to tunnel out used the dodge.

The years went past and Andy brought his wall out to the exercise yard cupful by cupful. He played the game with administrator after administrator, and they thought it was because he wanted to keep the library growing. I have no doubt that was part of it, but the main thing Andy wanted was to keep Cell 14 in Cellblock 5 a single occupancy.

I doubt if he had any real plans or hopes of breaking out, at least not at first. He probably assumed the wall was ten feet of solid concrete, and that if he succeeded in boring all the way through it, he'd come out thirty feet over the exercise yard. But like I say, I don't think he was worried overmuch about breaking through. His assumption could have run this way: I'm only making a foot of progress every seven years or so; therefore, it would take me seventy years to break through; that would make me one hundred and one years old.

Here's a second assumption I would have made, had I been Andy: that eventually I would be caught and get a lot of solitary time, not to mention a very large black mark on my record. After all, there was the regular weekly inspection and a surprise toss—which usually came at night—every second week or so. He must have decided that things couldn't go on for long. Sooner or later, some screw was going to peek behind Rita Hayworth just to make sure Andy didn't have a sharpened spoon-handle or some marijuana reefers Scotch-taped to the wall.

And his response to that second assumption must have been *To hell with it.* Maybe he even made a game out of it. How far in can I get before they find out? Prison is a goddam boring place, and the chance of being surprised by an unscheduled inspection in the middle of the night while he had his poster unstuck probably added some spice to his life during the early years.

And I do believe it would have been impossible for him to get away with it just on dumb luck. Not for twenty-seven years. Nevertheless, I have to believe that for the first two years—until mid-May of 1950, when he helped Byron Hadley get around the tax on his windfall inheritance—that's exactly what he did get by on.

Or maybe he had something more than dumb luck going for him even back then. He had money, and he might have been slipping someone a little squeeze every week to take it easy on him. Most guards will go along with that if the price is right; it's money in their pockets and the prisoner gets to keep his whack-off pictures or his tailormade cigarettes. Also, Andy was a model prisoner—quiet, well-spoken, respectful, non-violent. It's the crazies and the stampeders that get their cells turned upside-down at least once every six months, their mattresses unzipped, their pillows taken away and cut open, the outflow pipe from their toilets carefully probed.

Then, in 1950, Andy became something more than a model prisoner. In 1950, he became a valuable commodity, a murderer who did tax-returns better than H & R Block. He gave gratis estate-planning advice, set up tax-shelters, filled out loan applications (sometimes creatively). I can remember him sitting behind his desk in the library, patiently going over a car-loan agreement paragraph by paragraph with a screwhead who wanted to buy a used DeSoto, telling the guy what was good about the agreement and what was bad about it, explaining to him that it was possible to shop for a loan and not get hit quite so bad, steering him away from the finance companies, which in those days were sometimes little better than legal loan-sharks. When he'd finished, the screwhead started to put out his hand . . . and then drew it back to himself quickly. He'd forgotten for a moment, you see, that he was dealing with a mascot, not a man.

Andy kept up on the tax laws and the changes in the stock market, and so his usefulness didn't end after he'd been in cold storage for awhile, as it might have done. He began to get his library money, his running war with the sisters had ended, and nobody tossed his cell very hard. He was a good nigger.

Then one day, very late in the going—perhaps around October of 1967—the long-time hobby suddenly turned into something else. One night while he was in the hole up to his waist with Raquel Welch hanging down over his ass, the pick end of his rock-hammer must have suddenly sunk into concrete past the hilt.

He would have dragged some chunks of concrete back, but maybe he heard others falling down into that shaft, bouncing back and forth, clinking off that standpipe. Did he know by then that he was going to come upon that shaft, or was he totally surprised? I don't know. He might have seen the prison blueprints by then or he might not have. If not, you can be damned sure he found a way to look at them not long after.

All at once he must have realized that, instead of just playing a game, he was playing for high stakes . . . in terms of his own life and his own future, the highest. Even then he couldn't have known for sure, but he must have had a pretty good idea because it was right around then that he talked to me about Zihuatanejo for the first time. All of a sudden, instead of just being a toy, that stupid hole in the wall became his master—if he knew about the sewer-pipe at the bottom, and that it led under the outer wall, it did, anyway.

He'd had the key under the rock in Buxton to worry about for years. Now he had to worry that some eager-beaver new guard would look behind his poster and expose the whole thing, or that he would get another cellmate, or that he would, after all those years, suddenly be transferred. He had all those things on his mind for the next eight years. All I can say is that he must have been one of the coolest men who ever lived. I would have gone completely nuts after awhile, living with all that uncertainty. But Andy just went on playing the game.

He had to carry the possibility of discovery for another eight years—the *probability* of it, you might say, because no matter how carefully he stacked the cards in his favor, as an inmate of a state prison, he just didn't have that many to stack . . . and the gods had been kind to him for a very long time; some nineteen years.

The most ghastly irony I can think of would have been if he had been offered a parole. Can you imagine it? Three days before the parolee is actually released, he is transferred into the light security wing to undergo a complete physical and a battery of vocational tests. While he's there, his old cell is completely cleaned out. Instead of getting his parole, Andy would have gotten a long turn downstairs in solitary, followed by some more time upstairs . . . but in a different cell.

If he broke into the shaft in 1967, how come he didn't escape until 1975?

I don't know for sure—but I can advance some pretty good guesses.

First, he would have become more careful than ever. He was too smart to just push ahead at flank speed and try to get out in eight months, or even in eighteen. He must have gone on widening the opening on the crawlspace a little at a time. A hole as big as a teacup by the time he took his New Year's Eve drink that year. A hole as big as a dinner-plate by the time he took his birthday drink in 1968. As big as a serving-tray by the time the 1969 baseball season opened.

For a time I thought it should have gone much faster than it apparently did—after he broke through, I mean. It seemed to me that, instead of having to pulverize the crap and take it out of his cell in the cheater gadgets I have described, he could simply let it drop down the shaft. The length of time he took makes me believe that he didn't dare do that. He might have decided that the noise would arouse someone's suspicions. Or, if he knew about the sewer-pipe, as I believe he must have, he would have been afraid that a falling chunk of concrete would break it before he was ready, screwing up the cellblock sewage system and leading to an investigation. And an investigation, needless to say, would lead to ruin.

Still and all, I'd guess that, by the time Nixon was sworn in for his second term, the hole would have been wide enough for him to wriggle through . . . and probably sooner than that. Andy was a small guy.

Why didn't he go then?

That's where my educated guesses run out, folks; from this point they become progressively wilder. One possibility is that the crawlspace itself was clogged with crap and he had to clear it out. But that wouldn't account for all the time. So what was it?

I think that maybe Andy got scared.

I've told you as well as I can how it is to be an institutional man. At first you can't stand those four walls, then you get so you can abide them, then you get so you accept them . . . and then, as your body and your mind and your spirit adjust to live on an HO scale, you get to love them. You are told when to eat, when you can write letters, when you can smoke. If you're at work in the laundry or the plate-shop, you're assigned five minutes of each hour when you can go to the bathroom. For thirty-five years, my time was twenty-five minutes after the hour, and after thirty-five years, that's the only time I ever felt the need to take a piss or have a crap; twenty-five minutes past the hour. And if for some reason I couldn't go, the need would pass at thirty after, and come back at twenty-five past the next hour.

I think Andy may have been wrestling with that tiger— that institutional syndrome—and also with the bulking fears that all of it might have been for nothing.

How many nights must he have lain awake under his poster, thinking about that sewer line, knowing that the one chance was all he'd ever get? The blueprints might have told him how big the pipe's bore was, but a blueprint couldn't tell him what it would be like inside that pipe—if he would be able to breathe without choking, if the rats were big enough and mean enough to fight instead of retreating . . . and a blueprint couldn't've told him what he'd find at the end of the pipe, when and if he got there. Here's a joke even funnier than the parole would have been: Andy breaks into the sewer line, crawls through five hundred yards of choking, shit-smelling darkness, and comes up against a heavy-gauge mesh screen at the end of it. Ha, ha, very funny.

That would have been on his mind. And if the long shot actually came in and he was able to get out, would he be able to get some civilian clothes and get away from the vicinity of the prison undetected? Last of all, suppose he got out of the pipe, got away from Shawshank before the alarm was raised, got to Buxton, overturned the right rock . . . and found nothing beneath? Not necessarily something so dramatic as arriving at the right field and discovering that a highrise apartment building had been erected on the spot, or that it had been turned into a supermarket parking lot. It could have been that some little kid who liked rocks noticed that piece of volcanic glass, turned it over, saw the deposit-box key, and took both it and the rock back to his room as souvenirs. Maybe a November hunter kicked the rock, left the key exposed, and a squirrel or a crow with a liking for bright shiny things had taken it away. Maybe there had been spring floods one year, breeching the wall, washing the key away. Maybe anything.

So I think—wild guess or not—that Andy just froze in place for awhile. After all, you can't lose if you don't bet. What did he have to lose, you ask? His library, for one thing. The poison peace of institutional life, for another. Any future chance to grab his safe identity.

But he finally did it, just as I have told you. He tried . . . and, my! Didn't he succeed in spectacular fashion? You tell me!

But *did* he get away, you ask? What happened after? What happened when he got to that meadow and turned over that rock . . . always assuming the rock was still there?

I can't describe that scene for you, because this institutional man is still in this institution, and expects to be for years to come.

But I'll tell you this. Very late in the summer of 1975, on September 15th, to be exact, I got a postcard which had been mailed from the tiny town of McNary, Texas. That town is on

the American side of the border, directly across from El Por-
venir. The message side of the card was totally blank. But I
know. I know it in my heart as surely as I know that we're all
going to die someday.

McNary was where he crossed. McNary, Texas.

So that's my story, Jack. I never believed how long it would
take to write it all down, or how many pages it would take. I
started writing just after I got that postcard, and here I am finishing up on January 14th, 1976. I've used three pencils right
down to knuckle-stubs, and a whole tablet of paper. I've kept
the pages carefully hidden . . . not that many could read my
hen-tracks, anyway.

It stirred up more memories than I ever would have believed.
Writing about yourself seems to be a lot like sticking a branch
into clear river-water and roiling up the muddy bottom.

Well, you weren't writing about yourself, I hear someone in the
peanut-gallery saying. *You were writing about Andy Dufresne.
You're nothing but a minor character in your own story.* But you
know, that's just not so. It's *all* about me, every damned word
of it. Andy was the part of me they could never lock up, the
part of me that will rejoice when the gates finally open for
me and I walk out in my cheap suit with my twenty dollars
of mad-money in my pocket. That part of me will rejoice no
matter how old and broken and scared the rest of me is. I guess
it's just that Andy had more of that part than me, and used it
better.

There are others here like me, others who remember Andy.
We're glad he's gone, but a little sad, too. Some birds are not
meant to be caged, that's all. Their feathers are too bright,
their songs too sweet and wild. So you let them go, or when
you open the cage to feed them they somehow fly out past you.
And the part of you that knows it was wrong to imprison them
in the first place rejoices, but still, the place where you live is
that much more drab and empty for their departure.

That's the story and I'm glad I told it, even if it is a bit inconclusive and even though some of the memories the pencil prodded up (like that branch poking up the river-mud) made me feel a little sad and even older than I am. Thank you for listening. And Andy, if you're really down there, as I believe you are, look at the stars for me just after sunset, and touch the sand, and wade in the water, and feel free.

I never expected to take up this narrative again, but here I am with the dog-eared, folded pages open on the desk in front of me. Here I am adding another three or four pages, writing in a brand-new tablet. A tablet I bought in a store—I just walked into a store on Portland's Congress Street and bought it.

I thought I had put finish to my story in a Shawshank prison cell on a bleak January day in 1976. Now it's May of 1977 and I am sitting in a small, cheap room of the Brewster Hotel in Portland, adding to it.

The window is open, and the sound of the traffic floating in seems huge, exciting, and intimidating. I have to look constantly over at the window and reassure myself that there are no bars on it. I sleep poorly at night because the bed in this room, as cheap as the room is, seems much too big and luxurious. I snap awake every morning promptly at six-thirty, feeling disoriented and frightened. My dreams are bad. I have a crazy feeling of free fall. The sensation is as terrifying as it is exhilarating.

What has happened in my life? Can't you guess? I was paroled. After thirty-eight years of routine hearings and routine denials (in the course of those thirty-eight years, three lawyers died on me), my parole was granted. I suppose they decided that, at the age of fifty-eight, I was finally used up enough to be deemed safe.

I came very close to burning the document you have just read. They search outgoing parolees almost as carefully as they search incoming "new fish." And beyond containing enough dynamite to assure me of a quick turnaround and another six or eight years inside, my "memoirs" contained something else: the name of the town where I believe Andy Dufresne to be. Mexican police gladly cooperate with the American police, and I didn't want my freedom—or my unwillingness to give up the story I'd worked so long and hard to write—to cost Andy his.

Then I remembered how Andy had brought in his five hundred dollars back in 1948, and I took out my story of him the same way. Just to be on the safe side, I carefully rewrote each page which mentioned Zihuatanejo. If the papers had been found during my "outside search," as they call it at The Shank, I would have gone back in on turnaround . . . but the cops would have been looking for Andy in a Peruvian sea-coast town named Las Intrudres.

The Parole Committee got me a job as a "stock-room assistant" at the big FoodWay Market at the Spruce Mall in South Portland—which means I became just one more ageing bagboy. There's only two kinds of bag-boys, you know; the old ones and the young ones. No one ever looks at either kind. If you shop at the Spruce Mall FoodWay, I may have even taken your groceries out to your car . . . but you'd have had to have shopped there between March and April of 1977, because that's as long as I worked there.

At first I didn't think I was going to be able to make it on the outside at all. I've described prison society as a scaled-down model of your outside world, but I had no idea of how *fast* things moved on the outside; the *raw speed* people move at. They even talk faster. And louder.

It was the toughest adjustment I've ever had to make, and I haven't finished making it yet . . . not by a long way. Women, for instance. After hardly knowing that they were half of the human race for forty years, I was suddenly working in a store filled with them. Old women, pregnant women wearing tee-shirts with arrows pointing downward and a printed motto reading BABY HERE, skinny women with their nipples poking out at their shirts—a woman wearing something like that when I went in would have gotten arrested and then had a sanity hearing—women of every shape and size. I found myself going around with a semi-hard almost all the time and cursing myself for being a dirty old man.

Going to the bathroom, that was another thing. When I had to go (and the urge always came on me at twenty-five past the hour), I had to fight the almost overwhelming need to check it with my boss. Knowing that was something I could just go and do in this too-bright outside world was one thing; adjusting my inner self to that knowledge after all those years of checking it with the nearest screwhead or facing two days in solitary for the oversight . . . that was something else.

My boss didn't like me. He was a young guy, twenty-six or -seven, and I could see that I sort of disgusted him, the way a cringing, servile old dog that crawls up to you on its belly to be petted will disgust a man. Christ, I disgusted myself. But . . . I couldn't make myself stop. I wanted to tell him: *That's what a whole life in prison does for you, young man. It turns everyone in a position of authority into a master, and you into every master's dog. Maybe you know you've become a dog, even in prison, but since everyone else in gray is a dog, too, it doesn't seem to matter so much. Outside, it does.* But I couldn't tell a young guy like him. He would never understand. Neither would my PO, a big, bluff ex-Navy man with a huge red beard and a large stock of Polish jokes. He saw me for about five minutes every week. "Are you staying out of the bars, Red?" he'd ask when he'd run out of Polish jokes. I'd say yeah, and that would be the end of it until next week.

Music on the radio. When I went in, the big bands were just getting up a good head of steam. Now every song sounds like it's about fucking. So many cars. At first I felt like I was taking my life into my hands every time I crossed the street.

There was more—*everything* was strange and frightening—

but maybe you get the idea, or can at least grasp a corner of it. I began to think about doing something to get back in. When you're on parole, almost anything will serve. I'm ashamed to say it, but I began to think about stealing some money or shoplifting stuff from the FoodWay, anything, to get back in where it was quiet and you knew everything that was going to come up in the course of the day.

If I had never known Andy, I probably would have done that. But I kept thinking of him, spending all those years chipping patiently away at the cement with his rock-hammer so he could be free. I thought of that and it made me ashamed and I'd drop the idea again. Oh, you can say he had more reason to be free than I did—he had a new identity and a lot of money. But that's not really true, you know. Because he didn't know for sure that the new identity was still there, and without the new identity, the money would always be out of reach. No, what he needed was just to be free, and if I kicked away what I had, it would be like spitting in the face of everything he had worked so hard to win back.

So what I started to do on my time off was to hitchhike rides down to the little town of Buxton. This was in the early April of 1977, the snow just starting to melt off the fields, the air just beginning to be warm, the baseball teams coming north to start a new season playing the only game I'm sure God approves of. When I went on these trips, I carried a Silva compass in my pocket.

There's a big hayfield in Buxton, Andy had said, *and at the north end of that hayfield there's a rock wall, right out of a Robert Frost poem. And somewhere along the base of that wall is a rock that has no earthly business in a Maine hayfield.*

A fool's errand, you say. How many hayfields are there in a small rural town like Buxton? Fifty? A hundred? Speaking from personal experience, I'd put it at even higher than that, if you add in the fields now cultivated which might have been haygrass when Andy went in. And if I did find the right one,

I might never know it. Because I might overlook that black piece of volcanic glass, or, much more likely, Andy put it into his pocket and took it with him.

So I'd agree with you. A fool's errand, no doubt about it. Worse, a dangerous one for a man on parole, because some of those fields were clearly marked with no trespassing signs. And, as I've said, they're more than happy to slam your ass back inside if you get out of line. A fool's errand . . . but so is chipping at a blank concrete wall for twenty-seven years. And when you're no longer the man who can get it for you and just an old bag-boy, it's nice to have a hobby to take your mind off your new life. My hobby was looking for Andy's rock.

So I'd hitchhike to Buxton and walk the roads. I'd listen to the birds, to the spring runoff in the culverts, examine the bottles the retreating snows had revealed—all useless non-returnables, I am sorry to say; the world seems to have gotten awfully spendthrift since I went into the slam—and look for hayfields.

Most of them could be eliminated right off. No rock walls. Others had rock walls, but my compass told me they were facing the wrong direction. I walked these wrong ones anyway. It was a comfortable thing to be doing, and on those outings I really *felt* free, at peace. An old dog walked with me one Saturday. And one day I saw a winter-skinny deer.

Then came April 23rd, a day I'll not forget even if I live another fifty-eight years. It was a balmy Saturday afternoon, and I was walking up what a little boy fishing from a bridge told me was called The Old Smith Road. I had taken a lunch in a brown FoodWay bag, and had eaten it sitting on a rock by the road. When I was done I carefully buried my leavings, as my dad taught me before he died, when I was a sprat no older than the fisherman who had named the road for me.

Around two o'clock I came to a big field on my left. There was a stone wall at the far end of it, running roughly north-west. I walked back to it, squelching over the wet ground, and began to walk the wall. A squirrel scolded me from an oak tree.

Three-quarters of the way to the end, I saw the rock. No mistake. Black glass and as smooth as silk. A rock with no earthly business in a Maine hayfield. For a long time I just looked at it, feeling that I might cry, for whatever reason. The squirrel had followed me, and it was still chattering away. My heart was beating madly.

When I felt I had myself under control, I went to the rock, squatted beside it—the joints in my knees went off like a double-barrelled shotgun—and let my hand touch it. It was real. I didn't pick it up because I thought there would be anything under it; I could just as easily have walked away without finding what was beneath. I certainly had no plans to take it away with me, because I didn't feel it was mine to take—I had a feeling that taking that rock from the field would have been the worst kind of theft. No, I only picked it up to feel it better, to get the heft of the thing, and, I suppose, to prove its reality by feeling its satiny texture against my skin.

I had to look at what was underneath for a long time. My eyes saw it, but it took awhile for my mind to catch up. It was an envelope, carefully wrapped in a plastic bag to keep away the damp. My name was written across the front in Andy's clear script.

I took the envelope and left the rock where Andy had left it, and Andy's friend before him.

Dear Red,

If you're reading this, then you're out. One way or another, you're out. And if you've followed along this far, you might be willing to come a little further. I think you remember the name of the town, don't you? I could use a good man to help me get my project on wheels.

Meantime, have a drink on me—and do think it over. I will be keeping an eye out for you. Remember that

hope is a good thing, Red, maybe the best of things, and
no good thing ever dies. I will be hoping that this letter
finds you, and finds you well.

Your friend,
Peter Stevens

I didn't read that letter in the field. A kind of terror had
come over me, a need to get away from there before I was seen.
To make what may be an appropriate pun, I was in terror of
being apprehended.

I went back to my room and read it there, with the smell of
old men's dinners drifting up the stairwell to me—Beefaroni,
Rice-a-Roni, Noodle Roni. You can bet that whatever the old
folks of America, the ones on fixed incomes, are eating tonight,
it almost certainly ends in *roni.*

I opened the envelope and read the letter and then I put my
head in my arms and cried. With the letter there were twenty
new fifty-dollar bills.

And here I am in the Brewster Hotel, technically a fugitive
from justice again—parole violation is my crime. No one's
going to throw up any roadblocks to catch a criminal wanted
on that charge, I guess—wondering what I should do now.

I have this manuscript. I have a small piece of luggage
about the size of a doctor's bag that holds everything I own. I
have nineteen fifties, four tens, a five, three ones, and assorted
change. I broke one of the fifties to buy this tablet of paper and
a deck of smokes.

Wondering what I should do.

But there's really no question. It always comes down to just
two choices. Get busy living or get busy dying.

First I'm going to put this manuscript back in my bag.
Then I'm going to buckle it up, grab my coat, go downstairs,
and check out of this fleabag. Then I'm going to walk uptown
to a bar and put that five-dollar bill down in front of the bar-

tender and ask him to bring me two straight shots of Jack Daniel's—one for me and one for Andy Dufresne. Other than a beer or two, they'll be the first drinks I've taken as a free man since 1938. Then I am going to tip the bartender a dollar and thank him kindly. I will leave the bar and walk up Spring Street to the Greyhound terminal there and buy a bus ticket to El Paso by way of New York City. When I get to El Paso, I'm going to buy a ticket to McNary. And when I get to McNary, I guess I'll have a chance to find out if an old crook like me can find a way to float across the border and into Mexico.

Sure I remember the name. Zihuatanejo. A name like that is just too pretty to forget.

I find I am excited, so excited I can hardly hold the pencil in my trembling hand. I think it is the excitement that only a free man can feel, a free man starting a long journey whose conclusion is uncertain.

I hope Andy is down there.

I hope I can make it across the border.

I hope to see my friend and shake his hand.

I hope the Pacific is as blue as it has been in my dreams.

I *hope*.

About the Author

Stephen King is the author of more than sixty books, all of them worldwide bestsellers. His recent work includes *If It Bleeds*; *The Institute*; *Elevation*; *The Outsider*; *Sleeping Beauties* (co-written with his son Owen King); and the Bill Hodges Trilogy—*Mr. Mercedes*, *Finders Keepers*, and *End of Watch*. He is the recipient of the 2018 PEN America Literary Service Award and the 2014 National Medal of Arts. He lives in Bangor, Maine, with his wife, novelist Tabitha King.